"Come b

His eyes searched her face and she flashed hot and cold. They both knew they were talking about more than another kiss.

"Sure," he said without smiling.

They hardly spoke as the taxi sped through the inky, neon-splashed streets. They were too tense, too burning, too anxious. Camille kept stealing little glances Jonno's way and every time she saw him, she felt completely overwhelmed. This was Jonno Rivers, the most desirable of all *Girl Talk*'s heartthrob bachelors.

And here he was in a taxi with her. *Coming back to her flat.*

Barbara Hannay was born in Sydney, educated in Brisbane and has spent most of her adult life living in tropical North Queensland, where she and her husband have raised four children. While she has enjoyed many happy times camping and canoeing in the bush, she also delights in an urban lifestyle—chamber music, contemporary dance, movies and dining out. An English teacher, she has always loved writing, and now, by having her stories published, she is living her most cherished fantasy.

Visit www.barbarahannay.com.

Barbara Hannay captures the terrifying uncertainty of falling in love, as well as butterflies-in-the-stomach attraction. *A Parisian Proposition* is compulsive reading—unpredictable, emotional and inspiring!

A PARISIAN PROPOSITION
Barbara Hannay

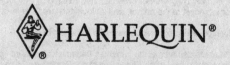

HARLEQUIN®

TORONTO • NEW YORK • LONDON
AMSTERDAM • PARIS • SYDNEY • HAMBURG
STOCKHOLM • ATHENS • TOKYO • MILAN • MADRID
PRAGUE • WARSAW • BUDAPEST • AUCKLAND

ISBN 0-373-03770-8

A PARISIAN PROPOSITION

First North American Publication 2003.

Visit us at www.eHarlequin.com

Printed in U.S.A.

CHAPTER ONE

'HEY, Jonno, there's a woman asking for you.'

Jonathan Rivers dragged his attention from a first-class pen of Angus steers and shot a quick sideways glance down the muddy alley of the cattle sale yards.

A woman, dressed in a pale city suit and high heels, hovered at the far end of the pens where the concrete path ended and the sloppy mud began.

He stifled an urge to curse. 'Not another husband-hunter?'

'I guess so,' Andy Bowen, his stock and station agent, admitted with a shrug. 'But this one's a cut above the rest. You should check her out, mate.'

Jonno groaned and shook his head in disbelief. 'I was hoping I wouldn't have to go through this again.'

'At least this one's got class,' chuckled Andy. 'And I reckon she's as stubborn as you are. Classy, sexy and stubborn as the devil. Could be your lucky day.'

'If you're so impressed, you go see what she wants.'

Andy winked. 'I've spoken to her and I know exactly what she wants.' He raised his voice to reach Jonno above the crescendo of the auctioneer's calls in the adjacent stall. 'She wants *you!*'

Against his better judgement, Jonno let his gaze slide sideways again. He caught a fleeting impression of contrasts—of a sophisticated female in smart city clothes amidst rough-clad country folk and cattle. A mass of exotic dark hair, dark eyes and dark mouth, set dramatically against pale skin. Physical slenderness offset by a proud carriage that hinted at inner strength.

She wants you.

'I'm not bloody available,' he growled.

'Course you're available. You've sold most of your cattle. I'll look after this last pen. I know the price you want for them. Get going, Jonno. You can't leave a lady like her in all that mud and cattle muck.'

The woman was still watching him intently and Jonno knew she would be aware that Andy had delivered her message. He let out a noisy sigh. 'I suppose I should be good at this rejection caper by now.'

Over the past months he'd literally lost count of the number of women who'd come chasing him since that crazy story turned up in the women's magazine. Blondes, brunettes, redheads and all shades in between…older women and young girls…plain, beautiful…cautious, reckless, polite…rude…

He'd sent them all packing…

As he strode grimly towards this latest contender his gumboots squelched in the mud. Recent rains and the pounding of thousands of cattle hooves had turned the dirt floor of the sale yards into a quagmire.

The woman, dressed in a soft beige wool suit with pale stockings and neat beige, high-heeled shoes, was eyeing the smelly mud warily as she waited for him at the edge of the walkway.

He surprised himself by slowing his steps as he drew near so he didn't splash her, but that was as far as his concessions went. He refused to smile. 'You're looking for me?'

'Yes.' She smiled cautiously and held out her hand. There was a small dark mole just above her upper lip. It was maddeningly distracting. 'How do you do, Mr Rivers? I'm Camille Devereaux.'

Her curly hair was dark chocolate and glossy, her eyes and lashes closer to black than brown, and her nose and chin were saved from sharpness by an indefinable elegance. Camille Devereaux. It occurred to Jonno that she matched her French name perfectly.

As he extended a brief, reluctant handshake, she studied him with disturbing directness, her gaze intensely curious and not at all shy.

And damn it, her perfume drifted towards him, teasing his senses for a tantalising instant before it was overpowered by the prevailing stench of mud and cattle.

Her hand in his felt soft and cool. Jonno snatched his own rough and callused hand away, shoved it into the back pocket of his jeans and tried to ignore the fact that Andy had been right.

This one was a cut above the others…

She had the intriguing allure of an exotic stranger. Very Mediterranean. Unexpectedly sexy.

His mistake was to allow his gaze to connect with hers for just a shade too long. For a fraction longer than was wise, he'd stared into her eyes and—

And hell. He'd never experienced anything like the sudden certainty that he and this stranger shared an unwilling reaction, that they'd both felt the same helpless stirring. A deep shudder inside.

An involuntary leap of awareness.

'Look,' he said quickly. Too quickly. Although Camille Devereaux hadn't told him why she was here, and although she looked different, he knew she would be the same as all the others. 'I can't help you. There's been a mistake. The magazine got it wrong. I'm not looking for someone to date and I'm certainly not looking for a wife.' He whirled away. 'Sorry to disappoint.'

'No, don't go,' she cried.

But he kept walking. He'd done this countless times and it was always embarrassing.

'I've no intention of dating or marrying you,' she called loudly. Way too loudly.

The bunch of cattlemen who were gathered around the nearby pen of heifers swung their fascinated gazes from Jonno to Camille and back to Jonno and grinned like mad.

'Another one?' someone called. 'What's the count now, Jonno?'

Teeth gritted, Jonno refused to turn. He kept hurrying through the mud.

'Jonno!' she yelled. 'Mr Rivers, we've got to talk!'

There was a hint of desperation in that last cry but he didn't look back. There was nothing more to say. He'd delivered his message and he wasn't going to hang around chatting to a beautiful stranger while he fuelled the entire Mullinjim community with a month's worth of gossip and cheap laughs.

Camille blamed the lack of coffee.

That was why she'd stuffed up. It had never happened

before. She had never missed her mark. It was unprofessional.

It had nothing to do with meeting Jonathan Rivers in the flesh after weeks of trying to make contact. It was caffeine withdrawal that had made her hollow and shivery, brain-dead and tongue-tied. Not Jonno.

And it was lack of caffeine plus too much squelchy, smelly mud that had stopped her from running after the obstinate cattleman and forcing him to listen to her.

But what kind of experienced, hard-nosed journalist was she if she let him get away before she'd had a chance to explain *anything*? To ask anything! OK, maybe thinking of herself as hard-nosed was over-the-top, but she was experienced and competent.

And yet she'd stood there like a ninny and watched him walk off without unearthing one measly reason for his lack of co-operation in 'The Bachelor Project'.

It had been so unreal...the way he'd looked at her...and...

She shook her head and shrugged. She'd lost it. For some reason, meeting Jonno had shrivelled her synapses. Which was pretty silly considering she'd seen his photo and had been expecting the magnetic intensity of his eyes, the rough, chiselled cheekbones and the dangerous mouth.

The heartthrob, half-mast smile.

It was his smile that had sealed Jonno Rivers's fate. Well...if she was honest...it was the crooked smile *and* the huge shoulders *and* the breathtaking fit of his low-slung jeans.

For the team at *Girl Talk* magazine, choosing

Jonathan Rivers for inclusion in 'The Pick of Australia's Eligible Bachelors' had been a no-brainer. And they'd decided that the pic he'd submitted was so good there was no need to send a professional photographer.

That had been *Girl Talk*'s first big mistake.

If they'd sent someone out at the beginning, Camille might have been saved this vexing journey now.

The second mistake had been Camille's. When she'd been put in charge of 'The Bachelor Project' she'd made a serious error of judgement. After selecting a range of bachelor volunteers from various walks of life, she'd taken the fellows she'd expected to be difficult as her personal responsibility—the high-powered lawyer from Perth, the owner of the construction company in Sydney and the executive chef in Melbourne.

She'd left the lower-profile contenders for more junior journalists to deal with—fellows like the tourist operator in Tasmania, the crocodile-hunter in the Northern Territory…and the cattleman in Queensland…

And it was only recently she'd discovered that the cattleman hadn't been playing the game.

Now she'd had to travel all the way from Sydney to North Queensland to get to the bottom of his problem and after several false leads she'd finally, *finally* tracked him down. And she'd barely managed three words of conversation before she'd let him go.

But if Jonno Rivers thought she'd give up after such a brief, unsatisfactory exchange, he was in for a nasty surprise. Or three.

It was her mission to tell him he couldn't back out of the bachelor story now. She wasn't going to let him wreck her magazine's project and she certainly wasn't going to let him jeopardise her job.

He might have refused to return phone calls, e-mail, faxes and letters. *And* he might have put padlocks on the gate to his cattle property, Edenvale, as she'd discovered this morning when she'd driven all the way out there.

She'd crawled along muddy outback roads while her little hire car scraped its underbelly on every bump, only to find his front gate one hundred per cent, in-her-face locked.

But she hadn't let smug, fat padlocks and rusty chains stop her.

And she hadn't been deterred when she tracked down Jonno's brother, Gabe, only to have him refuse to take her by helicopter over the locked gate and into Edenvale.

And now that she had tracked him down to these sale yards and had finally set eyes on the infamous and elusive Jonathan Rivers, she certainly wasn't going to let sloppy mud stop her! Not when she had knee-high boots and an oilskin coat in the back of her car.

She hurried back through the car park, where the sight of men on horseback and enormous road trains the size of locomotives with triple decks of cattle pens on the back rekindled the unsettling sense of alienation she'd felt ever since she'd arrived in Mullinjim.

It was weird. She'd always thought of herself as a true-blue Aussie, but this was her first trip from Sydney to the real outback and she couldn't have felt more of an outsider if she'd been on assignment in an exotic foreign country.

She was relieved that at least she was much less conspicuous when she prowled back through the disgusting mud of the sale yards camouflaged by her coat and boots.

Let Jonno hide. She would find him.

She scanned the lanes between the pens of bellowing cattle. Each lane was filled with cattlemen in look-alike wide-brimmed akubra hats, oilskin coats and jeans.

A sudden clomping of hooves forced her to turn and every organ in Camille's body lurched when she saw a mob of cattle being herded down the lane towards her by a man on horseback. Help! The beasts were massive and their hooves looked heavy and hard enough to crush and maim!

She'd never seen a cow that wasn't safely on the other side of a fence! And there were dozens of them bearing down on her. Some were snorting, others bellowing. Some had horns! Would there be enough room for them to pass?

Oh, God! Heart pounding, she squashed herself hard against the timber rails of the nearest pen, but even so one black beast eyeballed her fiercely as it drew close. She held her breath and squeezed in her stomach muscles, trying to flatten herself even more.

Glued to the fence like a fridge magnet, she felt her heart thrash. What would the girls in the office think if they could see her now? Surely this deserved some kind of bravery award. It was above and beyond the call of duty.

CITY GIRL SQUASHED FLAT BY FAT CATTLE...
Sydney journalist Camille Devereaux, faced a stam-

peding herd of wild beasts in the Mullinjim sale yards earlier today...*Vale*, Camille... Trampled to death while chasing a vital story for *Girl Talk* magazine...

She was so busy fighting her panic by composing more tributes to her bravery and courage that it was some time before it finally sank in that the animals were trotting past without paying her any particular attention. The man on horseback acknowledged her with a brief nod as he went by, then turned his mob into another lane.

Camille sagged against the pen as her breath escaped. She was still alive. She hadn't spooked the cattle. The guy on the horse had given her a casual nod as if she had every right to be here.

How about that? Her coat and boots must have done the trick. She looked as if she belonged. She felt inordinately pleased with herself.

Something nudged her elbow and she whipped around to discover a large, damp and very bovine nose sniffing her sleeve. Oh, God! The pen she'd been leaning against was full of another lot of cattle! She suppressed the urge to panic again. It was OK. These four-footed fellows were securely *inside* the pen. Nothing to worry about here. A snap.

She allowed a few minutes for her heartbeats to steady and her breathing to settle and realised that the pen she'd chosen to lean against was becoming a matter of some interest. Half a dozen or more cattlemen were joining her to stare over the fence at the beasts.

But the men hardly gave Camille a second glance.

Wow! This confirmation that she looked like a country girl gave her fresh confidence. Now she could track down Jonno Rivers through any amount of mud.

There was a rising babble of voices around her and the excited chanting of an auctioneer calling cattle prices. 'One-forty, one-forty! Hup! One-forty-five!'

She paid little attention. She was scanning the metal walkways above the pens for signs of Jonno and she thought she glimpsed him. This time she wouldn't let him go till she got what she'd come for.

Her view was blocked by the press of men around the pen and she stood on the bottom rung of the fence to get a better view. Above her, a promising set of shoulders and a slow, almost insolent stride came into her line of sight. Yes, it was Jonno.

'One-fifty-five!' the auctioneer's voice shouted.

She had no idea how to get up to that suspended walkway. If she could at least get Jonno's attention... Standing on tiptoes, she waved.

'Hup! One-sixty!'

Jonno was looking at a point just beyond her. She waved again.

'One-sixty twice!'

Camille glanced briefly in the direction of the strident voice. The auctioneer was standing on the same walkway as Jonno but directly above her, pointing straight at her. All around her, men were moving away from the pen, heading off down the lane.

A ghastly suspicion sent shivers chasing down her back and arms. No, he couldn't think that she—

'One-sixty!' the auctioneer shouted, staring straight at

her. 'Hup! I've got one-sixty! Going for one-sixty. Sold!'

'Congratulations,' said a voice at her side.

She whirled around to find the ruddy-faced man who'd fetched Jonno for her.

'Oh, good grief!' She gulped. 'You're not congratulating *me*, are you?'

His beaming, slice-of-watermelon smile widened. 'Sure am. You've bought a fine pen of weaner steers.'

'I have not!' She gasped. 'I can't have. Tell me you're joking.'

The man slapped his hand on the top rail of the pen. 'This mob of little beauties here. All yours.'

'But I was waving to Jonno Rivers. I...' She flashed a frantic glance back to the auctioneer, but he simply gave a curt salute to the man at her side, then headed towards another pen. 'It can't happen like that,' she spluttered. 'I'm not a genuine buyer. How—how on earth could he have thought I wanted a pen of cattle?'

'You were standing next to me.'

'What's that got to do with anything?'

'I'm a stock and station agent. Brian must have assumed you were one of my clients.'

'Oh, my God!' She pressed a shaking hand to her forehead. 'You'll go and tell him it's a mistake, won't you?'

'You don't want these steers?'

'Of course I don't want them.' She sent a scathing glance over the pen of cattle and let out a laughing groan. 'What on earth would I do with them? I live in a one-bedroom flat in Kings Cross. My courtyard is smaller than this pen.'

'You could put them out on agistment.'

A deep voice sounded at her back. 'Is this woman hassling you, Andy?'

Camille spun around to find a scowling Jonno Rivers close behind her. His suspicious gaze was cold enough to freeze an ocean. Two oceans.

'Jonno,' greeted the ever cheerful Andy. 'You're just the man we need.'

Camille wasn't so sure. She'd had about as much as she could take of this pesky cattleman and his sulky silence and his stinking cattle. Her fists curled against her thighs and she felt an overwhelming urge to thump him on the nose.

'This young lady seems to have a little problem,' the agent explained calmly. 'But I'm sure you can help her, mate.' He glanced at his watch. 'Sorry, Jonno, I've got to see a man about a bull. Catch you later.' With a brief salute, he hurried away.

Camille's stomach and head were spinning as she gaped after him. She felt exhausted as she turned back to Jonno. 'At least you've had the guts to show up,' she muttered. 'This is all your fault, so you'll have to do something about it.'

CHAPTER TWO

JONNO took ages to respond.

He stood with his long legs planted wide and his arms folded over his broad chest and he looked down at Camille without any sign of sympathy. 'Before you get too carried away with accusations,' he said at last, 'could you please explain what's going on?'

'I was simply waving at you,' she said. 'And...' She ran nervous fingers through her curls, annoyed by his air of remoteness.

'And?'

'And apparently I bought these cows.'

He glanced at the pen beside her. 'They're steers.'

'Cows, steers, whatever. They have four legs and they say "moo" and I don't want them.'

A muscle in his cheek twitched and he looked away, then heaved a deep sigh as he stared at something in the distance. 'I knew you were going to be more trouble than the others.'

'I beg your pardon?'

He swung his gaze back to settle coldly over her. 'Did you reckon I'd find you more attractive if you threw in a pen of steers as a bribe?'

Camille gaped at him. 'You think I bought them as some kind of...of bait—like a dowry? To make myself more appealing to *you*?'

17

He didn't reply, but a slight inclination of his head suggested an answer in the affirmative.

Where did this guy get off? He had an ego bigger than the outback! 'You really think I fancy you?'

His big shoulders moved in a faint shrug. 'You're trailing after me, aren't you?'

She had to shove her curling fists deep into her pockets before she did something really foolish. He was actually far too big to punch. 'How about you clean your ears out and listen, mate?' she said slowly and loudly and with what she felt was an impressive degree of menace. 'I came out here because you reneged on your agreement with *Girl Talk* magazine. I have absolutely no interest in you as a date.'

She flung her arms out in a wide, sweeping gesture to take in the mud and the cattle. 'Could you honestly believe I would be way out here splashing around in mud and muck if I had a choice? It's certainly not my idea of fun. As for boyfriends, I have as many guys in Sydney as I—as I need. And the last—the very last—kind of man I'm looking for is a cowboy!'

For good measure she added, 'And I haven't the slightest interest in getting married. Not ever. Not to anyone. In case you haven't caught up with the latest statistics, there's a whole generation of girls like me who are not desperate to sacrifice ourselves on the matrimonial altar.'

His obvious surprise gave her a measure of satisfaction. And for the first time she thought she saw a hint of amusement lurking in the depths of his hazel eyes.

'I think I believe you,' he said.

'Well, hallelujah!' Nodding towards the cattle, she finished her speech. 'You might also be able to accept the fact that buying these guys was a complete accident that's turned a rotten day for me into a total disaster.'

A suspicion of a smile played around his mouth. 'Did you pay a good price for them?'

'I wouldn't have a clue. But that's not the point.'

'It's very much the point. And so is whether or not you have the money to pay for them.'

'But I don't want them.' Camille scowled at him and then at the cattle standing meekly in their pen. 'I've no idea if I can afford them,' she admitted. 'How much are they?'

He shrugged. 'Fifteen weaner steers…at a good weight. I'd say you're looking at somewhere around six thousand dollars.'

'No way!' She suppressed an urge to add a few swear words. 'I'm saving for a trip to Paris and that's almost my entire savings! I'm not going to blow it on a pen of cattle.'

She'd been saving madly over the past twelve months. Hadn't bought any new clothes in all that time! Well…hardly any. And now her dreams were toppling like a collapsed football scrum.

All her lovely dreams…of travelling to see her father again after twelve long years, of discovering her favourite sculptures in the Musée Rodin, of hunting for exciting little cafés in the back streets of Montmartre, or buying something chic and extravagant on the Champs-Élysées…

In a few short minutes those dreams were gone, to be

replaced by a nightmare...a pen of fifteen weaner steers in outback Queensland.

Desperate, she rounded on Jonno. 'How can I get out of this?'

He shrugged his massive shoulders. 'I'm not sure.'

'Can I sue someone?'

'The vendor could probably sue you if you don't honour the bid.'

'Oh, hell!' Camille closed her eyes and tried to calm her rising panic. She needed to think clearly. There had to be a solution to this crazy situation. Her head was spinning. 'I can't think about this without coffee.'

'There's a canteen.'

She opened her eyes and squinted at him. 'Good. Let me shout you a coffee.' When he didn't answer, she added, 'Just coffee, Jonno. Not a date. Not a marriage proposal. I just want you on one side of a table, me on the other, a cup of coffee in my hand and a little market advice. If you were struggling to find a taxi in Sydney, or if you were out of your depth in Kings Cross, I'd do the same for you.'

He looked at her quizzically for a moment or two, but then to her relief he nodded. 'The canteen's this way.'

He led her down several muddy lanes lined with pens of bellowing beasts until they reached concrete paths and buildings that housed various administrative offices for the sale yards. After they scraped their boots on a rough outdoor mat, Jonno pushed open large glass doors.

Inside, the canteen was crowded with hungry cattlemen and their wives, but it was warm and clean and Camille could see a counter with shiny urns spouting steam and she could smell the fragrant aroma of coffee at last.

Jonno wouldn't let her pay and she accepted that country guys were probably still old-fashioned about things like that. With her hands wrapped around a warm mug, she inhaled the familiar aroma of her favourite beverage and took a quick, fortifying sip before they reached their table near a window in the corner. Jonno had bought two packets of sandwiches as well. Wholesome, grainy, country bread filled with cold roast meat, pickles and salad.

'So you want help to get rid of your cattle,' he said, once they were settled.

Camille nodded. 'Yes, please.' Then she took another deep sip of coffee before setting down her mug. 'You wouldn't like to buy them, would you?'

His mouth tilted into the familiar, crooked smile that had caused so much of a stir in the *Girl Talk* office. She noticed that the hazel in his eyes was a fascinating mixture of brown and gold with little flecks of green.

'No, thanks,' he said. 'I came to these sales today to sell, not to buy. It's not exactly a buyers' market.'

She sighed. So much for a simple, straightforward solution. 'Can I throw them right back on the market and sell them tomorrow?'

His smile faded as he looked thoughtful. 'It's possible… But before we get too worried about that, why don't you tell me why you've come all the way up here from Sydney?'

Camille's breath escaped on a gasp of surprise. Buying a pen of cattle had a good side? It got Jonno Rivers talking? Wow! She hadn't expected this breakthrough moment, but she might as well cut straight to the chase. 'I'm here to find out what game you're playing.'

'I'm not *playing* anything.'

'You know you've been playing games with our magazine. You haven't answered our letters or phone calls.'

He showed no sign of apology. 'Why should I co-operate with totally irresponsible journalism?'

'Irresponsible?' Her right eyebrow lifted, but she willed herself to stay calm. Now that she had him in her sights, she had to take extra care not to frighten him off. 'Why do you say that?'

'You expect me to fuel the dangerous illusions of a mob of silly, gullible women, who believe these bachelors you've unearthed are desperate for marriage and commitment.'

'We never gave the impression our bachelors are desperate. Heavens, Jonno, they're all heartthrobs.' After a beat, she added, 'Like you.'

He looked distinctly uncomfortable.

'We chose gorgeous, well-heeled guys, who for some reason—whether it's geographical isolation or twenty-four-seven commitment to their brilliant careers—are still single, but seeking a wife.'

When he didn't respond, she added, 'The reaction from readers has been amazing. We had no idea there were still so many women actively hunting for husbands.'

'Unlike you,' he challenged. 'That's another thing. How can someone who doesn't even believe in marriage pretend that it's so damn wonderful?'

'How do you know what I think of marriage?' Camille asked, then flinched. 'Oh, yeah. It was the seminal text of my sermon in the cattle stalls, wasn't it?'

She felt strangely caught out—embarrassed to realise that in the heat of the moment she'd aired her personal views about relationships to this man. This too, too sexy man.

She jabbed her finger at a piece of shredded lettuce that had fallen from her sandwich. 'So I take it there's been a mistake. You're as allergic to marriage as I am.'

'I never said I didn't want marriage.'

Her head jerked up. Jonno's eyes were an unsettling mixture of mild amusement and something else... something private and deep.

'But—'

'I don't have any hang-ups about marriage,' he said slowly. 'But when I choose a wife I'd like to do the chasing. Nothing turns me off faster than a woman who blatantly chases after me.'

Camille frowned. 'OK, so you'd better explain why on earth you agreed to take part in our project.'

His face grew hard and tight. 'I didn't.'

'Hello? I have a signed statement saying otherwise.'

A bleak shadow darkened his eyes and his mouth twisted bitterly. 'Look, I don't want to go into details about how I ended up in your magazine.'

'Are you saying...?' Camille pressed a hand to her stomach. Right from the very start she'd had a strange gut feeling that there'd been something a little different about Jonno's entry. 'Are you telling me that you were entered against your will?'

'Yes.'

'Framed?'

He nodded.

'So who sent us your photo? Your signature?'

'I told you I'm not prepared to give details, but, believe me, it was a mistake. A huge mistake.'

Camille was surprised by how readily she believed him. Nevertheless, the urge to press him for details was strong. In the past she'd never shied away from getting to the bottom of a story and she longed to know how a handsome devil like Jonathan Rivers could end up in *Girl Talk* by *mistake*. Her magazine and its readers deserved to know.

But even as the questions lined up in her head, something in his face stopped her from voicing them.

Her experience of interviewing people from all walks of life told her that the door on this particular conversation had clanged shut. It was locked as securely as the gate to his property, and she sensed that to pry would be useless—even dangerous. She could alienate him completely if she pushed too hard.

But her job was in jeopardy if she didn't.

'I don't think it's possible for you to simply bow out,' she told him. 'We can't retract you from the project now. Our readers are hanging out for the follow-up stories.'

'Of course you can drop me. I might have fallen under a bus. Anything's *possible*.'

'But you're one of our most popular bachelors.' In actual fact he was the most popular, but she decided nothing was to be gained by pumping up his ego more than necessary.

He glared at her. 'Too bad.'

As he drained his coffee, Camille's mind raced. If only she knew who had set Jonno up. Was it a practical joker? Or someone in town who had a grudge against him? A rejected lover? A misguided secret admirer?

His voice interrupted her thoughts. 'What's your position at *Girl Talk*?'

Her shoulders squared. 'I'm an associate editor.'

'How much say do you have?'

'In "The Bachelor Project"? It's my responsibility.' Now wasn't the moment to add that she still had to report to Edith King, the editor-in-chief.

Jonno sat without speaking for a long, thoughtful stretch of time, then he looked straight at her. 'Associate editor?' Resting both elbows on the table, he leaned towards her and his face was transformed by a slow smile. 'If you have enough clout as associate editor, I think we might be in a position to talk turkey, Camille Devereaux.'

Help! His smile was so wicked, so distracting, so devastating that she had to struggle to think straight. 'I'm sorry, I'm not on your wavelength.'

'I'm sure you are,' he said smoothly.

Was he flirting with her? No, of course he wasn't. Her brain had been short-circuited by that sexy smile and she was beginning to think like one of his groupies.

'We're both in an excellent position to help each other,' he prompted.

'We are?' She dropped her gaze. It would be easier to think when she wasn't trapped by that knockout smile. After a moment of staring at the remains of her abandoned sandwich, she felt the fuzz of foolishness clear. 'Oh, oh, yes, of course.' She looked up, suddenly worried. 'You're suggesting that if my magazine drops you from the bachelor project, you'll help me out with my cattle problem.'

'Exactly.'

Her thoughts flew to Edith. *Girl Talk*'s editor would have kittens if she heard that Jonathan Rivers was no longer part of the project. Then she thought of Paris. And of seeing her father. And of keeping her savings intact. 'How could you help me?' she asked, feeling her cheeks warm with growing excitement.

The smile lingered in his eyes. 'If I take your cattle out to my property at Edenvale, I could raise them for the next few months and then sell them on when the price is right and we can split the profits.'

'Profits?' The last thing she'd expected was to profit from his suggestion. 'You mean I could actually make some money from my little cows—I mean steers?'

'That's what we do to survive out here.'

'Could I make more than if I left my savings in the bank?'

'It's always an educated gamble, but we've had good summer rain and follow-up rain in late autumn. There's plenty of pasture in this district at the moment and, as long as the export prices continue to rise, we could make a tidy profit from your cattle.'

Her cattle. How weird that sounded. And yet Camille felt a little tremble of excitement, too, as if she was about to take the first tentative step towards a mysterious new adventure.

'But of course,' Jonno added, 'you'd have to promise to drop me out of your magazine.'

'Yes.' She bit her lip as she thought of the battle she would face when she got back to Sydney. Edith would probably rupture something. And Camille would have to find a way to soothe her. But she sensed that Jonno had valid reasons for wanting to be dropped from the bachelor project, and finding an excuse to cover for him would be a darn sight easier than finding someone else to look after her cattle. 'It's a deal,' she said, smiling back at him. 'Can we shake on that?'

For a moment he didn't respond. He sat staring at the tabletop, his expression deadly serious. 'Sure,' he said at last.

His strong hand gripped hers and their eyes met. And there was something so suddenly fiery and disturbing in his glance that it stole her breath. Her stomach seemed to fall from a great height.

Jonno quickly dropped his gaze and crumpled the greaseproof paper that had wrapped his sandwiches. 'OK. I'd better go and take care of the paperwork and I'll have a word with one of the truckies about getting that pen run out to Edenvale this afternoon.'

He stood and she realised that this was the end of their conversation.

Feeling absurdly disappointed, she reached into her shoulder bag and pulled out a business card. 'You'll need this if you want to contact me directly—about the cattle or…or anything.'

He frowned at the small card as he held it in his big hands, and he seemed to take ages as he scrutinised every item of her contact details. 'So you're heading back to Sydney?'

'I guess so,' she said, jumping to her feet. 'Although I probably won't make it to Townsville before dark tonight.'

He tapped the card against the tabletop. 'You should make it to Charters Towers. The road's pretty good and at least it's stopped raining. Then you could be in Townsville and catching a plane to Sydney by tomorrow morning.'

She nodded and hitched the strap of her bag over her shoulder. 'Thanks for lunch.'

'Pleasure.' He reached inside his coat, unbuttoned a little flap on his shirt pocket and slipped her card inside. There was an awkward, shades-of-high-school moment while they stood staring at each other without speaking. While she remembered that look in his eyes. Oh, crumbs, he was gorgeous.

He had to be one of the hunkiest guys she'd ever met, and that was an opinion shared by half the women in Australia. But, putting all that aside, now that she was on the point of departure, the spectre of her editor-in-chief's wrath loomed larger.

'Was there something else you wanted to discuss?' he asked when she didn't walk away. 'You're not having second thoughts, are you?'

She sighed. 'I can't help feeling I'm letting you wriggle out of this too easily.'

With a shake of his head, he released a scoffing, disbelieving laugh. 'How can you say that?'

'Well…all you have to do is put those calves into a

paddock and then you can relax with your feet up while they eat grass and grow fat and make easy money. Meanwhile, I have to face my boss and try to explain how I lost you from the project!'

To her surprise, he flushed dark red. His hands clenched and unclenched at his sides and he looked mad enough to grab her and shake her.

But he didn't move. He stood rock still, while his face slowly regained its natural colour and set into hard lines. His cheekbones looked more chiselled than ever and his eyes grew cold as marble. 'We struck a deal,' he said quietly. 'We shook hands. Maybe city folk haven't heard of a gentleman's agreement? But, sorry, there's no going back on it now.'

'I was afraid of that,' she said.

'How you keep up your end of the bargain is your problem.'

He marched out of the canteen without waiting for her response and without looking back.

Mullinjim was too remote for Camille's mobile phone to pick up the network, so she called Sydney from a phone box in the sale yard's car park.

'Oh, my God!' Edith shrieked. 'It's so good to hear from you, Camille. I've been fretting that we'd lost you in the outback! Did you make it to Mulla-what's-its-name?'

'Yes, I'm in Mullinjim, and I've been talking to Jonathan Rivers.'

'You little star! I knew you'd pull us out of this.'

Camille grimaced. 'Yeah—well—'

'I've been so stressed about our reluctant cowboy. He's the key to the whole project.'

'Edith, I've got to tell you it hasn't been easy. I'm afraid I've had to strike a kind of a—a deal with him.'

'OK, OK. We'll do whatever we've got to as long as we secure his story.'

'But—'

'No rampant cheque-book journalism, mind you. Don't go overboard, Camille. If he wants big money, he'll have to deal directly with me. Let me do the negotiating.'

Camille heard the faint click of a cigarette lighter on the other end of the line. Edith scorned rules about smoking in the office and Camille could picture her boss's long white fingers with their bright red nails lifting a cigarette to her painted lips.

'Edith, you don't understand. It's nothing to do with money.'

'Oh, my God, he wants to sleep with you?'

'*No!*' Camille sank against the side of the phone box and pressed a hand to her forehead. This was going to be even harder than she'd feared. 'He's simply not available.'

'*He's already married?*' Edith screeched.

'No, listen to me. It's all been a *mistake.*'

'He's not gay.' Edith groaned. 'Camille, tell me our cowboy's not gay.'

'He's not gay.' That was one thing she was sure of. Jonno had shown too much interest; she'd caught him checking her out too many times. But Camille almost flinched as she added, 'The mistake was that he never agreed to be part of the project in the first place.'

This was greeted by silence. Stony, bristling silence. Camille could picture Edith drawing deeply on her cigarette as the news sank in. She fancied she heard her exhale.

'Repeat that very slowly,' Edith said, her voice dropping several decibels but sounding twice as threatening. 'I hope I misheard you.'

Camille gulped. 'The bottom line is he wants out and I don't know if we can hold him.'

Suddenly she wished she could offer Edith a definite, valid reason. If only she'd forced Jonno to give her concrete evidence that he'd been framed.

'I'll explain when I'm back in Sydney, but he's completely uncooperative, Edith. I'm sorry. I did my best. You know I don't give up easily, but I hit a brick wall. We're not going to get anything out of him, so I'm on my way back. I should be home by tomorrow night.'

'Camille,' Edith thundered, her voice at full throttle again, 'you're not going anywhere. You'll stay right there, my dear, and you'll get me the Jonathan Rivers story.'

'But I told you—'

'I don't care what you have to do.' There was a brief pause while Edith let out a deep, noisy breath. 'You know I don't like making wild threats. Our relationship's above that. But there's more going on with the publishers than you realise and it's vital—you'd better believe me when I say it's *vital*, honey—that we pull this one off. Now, you get back to work on this lonesome cowboy. I'll expect a call tomorrow night with an update.'

She hung up.

Oh, help! I'm dead meat.

Camille dropped the receiver into the cradle and covered her face with her hands. She was toast. She'd already struck her bargain with Jonno, *her gentleman's agreement*, and her parting attempt to renegotiate had made him so furious she'd left herself no room to manoeuvre.

How on earth could she accommodate Jonathan Rivers's insistence on privacy *and* satisfy her editor?

Pushing the door of the phone box open, she stepped outside. Despite bright sunshine, a chill, wintry gust whipped at her coat and she dug her hands deep into her pockets and began to pace. She often thought better when she was walking.

What could she do? Dig until she found the truth behind Jonno's entry into the project? Would that really help? Perhaps her only hope was to come up with a great alternative story. If she could write a top piece of journalism…about life on a cattle station, perhaps…a woman's perspective about a cattleman's world…

She'd include thoughts about romance and marriage…a 'City Girl in the Bush' story…

Her enthusiasm warmed a little as her imagination kicked in. She'd have to make it good. She'd have to knock their socks off.

Hands deep in his coat pockets, Jonno stomped through the parking area next to the sale yards, trying to shake off his anger. Camille Devereaux's parting comment about the laid-back, effortless life of a cattleman had him riled. *Easy money be damned!*

He knew he shouldn't let anything she said bother him. She didn't have a clue about what was involved in raising cattle. She was an airhead from the city who didn't know squat about the way he earned a living—couldn't even tell a cow from a steer.

And she called herself a journalist?

But he shouldn't have let her go without setting her straight. He should have taken her outside that canteen and given her an earful...

Or kissed her senseless.

He stopped pacing. Was *that* his problem? Would he have cared two hoots what Camille thought if he hadn't found her so damned attractive? Was he angry because of what she said, or because of the way she looked?

Because he'd wanted her and couldn't have her?

Damn. He couldn't stop thinking about her dark hair and dark eyes. She had the intriguing allure of a beautiful stranger. Someone from another world. So exotic...

So what?

She was on her way back to Sydney. She was heading back to the city, full of her smug assumptions, and he'd missed his opportunity to set her straight, to let her know in no uncertain terms just how misinformed she was about a cattleman's life.

Camille rounded a mud-splattered four-wheel-drive vehicle and came to a halt as she saw Jonno pacing just a few metres away. He'd turned up the collar of his coat as protection from the wind and his dark hair was ruffled. Her heart thudded painfully as he looked up, saw her and stared fiercely.

His face was so dark and intimidating that she almost mumbled a quick hi-and-goodbye and hurried away, but Edith's commands were still ringing in her ears.

Sidestepping a puddle, she walked towards him. 'I was hoping I'd find you.'

He continued to scowl. 'Why? I thought you were leaving.'

'I've realised that I should make the most of my trip and do a story about outback life while I'm out here.'

His upper lip curled. 'And how are you going to do that? By describing the view from your motel window?'

'Of course not. I want to do an in-depth feature about the real outback.'

Jonno muttered what sounded like a curse and plunged his hands deep in his pockets. 'You'd be the last person to write about anything that resembles real life in the bush.'

'And what would you know? I'm a damn good journalist.'

'Don't kid yourself, Ms Devereaux. You turn up here. You stumble around a sale yard all starry-eyed and woolly-headed—and accidentally buy a pen of steers. Then you lump your mistakes on me and have the effrontery to talk about cattle-raising as easy money.'

Ah, she thought. I've dented that gigantic ego of his. 'I'm sorry. That was a thoughtless comment.'

He seemed surprised by her apology. For a moment his unsmiling eyes rested on her and they seemed to focus directly on her mouth. Her heart nearly stopped. Then he pulled his gaze upwards and looked her squarely in the eye. 'From what I've seen of your fancy magazine, you prefer fluff and nonsense. I don't recall an ounce of realism.'

Her chin lifted. 'Then give me realism.'

'In what form?'

'Give me a story, Jonno. Show me what your life is really like.'

He glowered at her. 'I don't want to be featured in any story you write.'

'I've promised I won't do a story about you as an eligible bachelor, but let me write one about your life out here. If you like I can emphasise how *un*-romantic the bush is for women.'

Holding up her hands as if to stop his flow of protests, she said, 'You won't be mentioned. I'll keep it anonymous—a general story about real life on a cattle property, a picture of what's expected of a woman or a wife in the bush from a city girl's point of view.'

'Which means a patronising, naive point of view.'

She gasped, stung by his words. How could someone so gorgeous be such an arrogant, chauvinist pig? 'OK, you win! Forget I ever asked! I'll find someone who doesn't have a huge grudge against the world beyond his doorstep!'

Swinging away from him, she stormed across the car park.

'Camille!'

A hard hand gripped her elbow, but she jerked her arm free and hurried on.

'Camille, wait, damn it!'

The grip was stronger this time and she was forced to stop and turn around.

'What do you want?'

To her surprise, Jonno was looking just a little shame-faced. 'I guess you weren't to know I was conned into that bachelor business, so I do owe you some kind of a story.'

'Don't trouble yourself. I can find any number of friendly, co-operative people. You seem to be the only person out here lacking in the famous bush hospitality we hear so much about.'

'Listen! If you want to do a story about a cattle prop-erty, you'd better come out to Edenvale.'

'To your place?' She knew her mouth was hanging open as his suggestion sank in.

'Yeah.'

'You mean you're actually inviting me through that locked gate to the inner sanctum?'

The shadow of a smile lightened his features, but then it was gone again as if whipped away by the wind.

'Are you sure?' she asked. It seemed impossible that the intransigent Jonno should make such an about-face.

He shrugged. 'If you're my business partner, you should take an interest in the well-being of your live-stock.'

She'd never thought of that angle. 'I guess I should.'

'You can see how the steers you've bought settle in.'

'Great.'

'They've just been weaned. They were still with their

mothers yesterday, so they'll be highly stressed and they'll need gentle handling when they arrive.'

'Really? The poor babies.' Cocking her head to one side, she hid her surprise behind a teasing smile. 'I hadn't realised you were such a Sensitive New Age Cowperson, Jonno.'

His jaw stiffened, but apart from that he ignored her dig and asked smoothly, 'Are you interested in my offer?'

'Yes, yes, of course I am.' She could write about her cattle. Already she could see her story taking shape. 'From City Girl to Cattle Queen in 5 Easy Steps.' Resisting the temptation to smile coyly, she kept her face deadpan as she added, 'I'd be fascinated to learn more about your techniques for gentle handling.'

CHAPTER THREE

JONNO'S brother, Gabe, rang about an hour after he arrived home with Camille.

'I thought I'd better warn you there's a journalist from that Sydney magazine snooping around town. She was in our office this morning looking for you.'

'Yeah. I know about her.'

'Did you know she tried to get me to chopper her into Edenvale?'

'Look, thanks for the warning, big brother, but actually you're too late. She's already found me.'

There was a beat of silence on the other end of the line. 'I hope you weren't too tough on her.'

Jonno cleared his throat. 'Course I wasn't. We—uh—worked things out—uh—more or less amicably.'

'Glad to hear you behaved yourself,' Gabe said. 'You've been so uptight about this magazine caper I had visions of a full-on brawl. It's a relief to hear she's still in one piece.'

Jonno winced. What would Gabe think if he knew that not only was Camille Devereaux in one piece, she was relaxing in a deep cane lounger on his back veranda, watching the sunset while Megs, his ginger tabby, purred on her lap and Saxon, his golden Labrador, sprawled across her feet?

He'd been crazy to bring her back here, but he blamed

his upbringing. His mother had instilled in both himself and Gabe an innate sense of courtesy.

Only a shabby barbarian could have continued with the sustained rudeness he'd extended towards this woman. He'd never behaved that way before and he'd felt compelled to compensate.

But too late he was realising what a big mistake he'd made by inviting her to Edenvale.

'It's a pity you couldn't have met that girl under more pleasant circumstances,' Gabe commented. 'Even a safely married man like me noticed that she's rather easy on the eye.'

'You reckon?' Jonno muttered, and felt his face heat. *Not* noticing how attractive Camille was had become the major challenge of the day.

He should have followed his initial instincts and refused to have anything to do with her. But he'd made mistake after flaming mistake.

And now she was home with him and had exchanged her tailored city suit for an old pair of jeans and a crimson, super-soft woollen sweater that outlined all too clearly the shapeliness of her breasts, and not looking at her had zoomed to an even higher level of difficulty.

'By the way,' Gabe said, 'Jim Young, the truckie, asked me to pass on a message. He says he's been held up at Piebald Downs and he won't get those steers through to you till later this evening.'

'OK. Thanks.'

'I didn't realise you were buying today,' Gabe commented. 'I thought you were selling. The prices weren't too good for buyers this week.'

'Yeah, well—slight change of plan.' Jonno sighed. It wasn't worth trying to keep secrets from his brother. He and his wife, Piper, lived right next door on Windaroo Station and, knowing the way gossip spread in the bush, it wouldn't be long before they found out about Camille's purchase. 'Camille bought one pen of steers.'

'Who's Camille?'

'The journalist. It's a long story, mate, but she bought them this morning and she's putting them here on agistment.'

'You're joking?'

''Fraid not. And you might as well know, she's staying here for a day or two.'

This was greeted by stunned silence from Gabe.

'It's part of a deal—a business deal we've struck,' said Jonno.

'That's—that's—fascinating.'

Jonno groaned. He knew Gabe was itching to ask a load of questions, so he rushed to explain. 'There's nothing fascinating about it, but she wants to write a piece for her magazine and I don't want her to sail back to Sydney telling the world that all I have to do is stick her steers in a paddock and then put my feet up. I'm going to show her a thing or two about the realities of country life.'

'Excellent.' Gabe chuckled. 'They're fine, noble motives, mate.'

'Motives? What do you mean?'

'Oh, nothing.' Gabe's voice rippled with suppressed laughter. 'After you've spent so long giving women the

brush-off, I'm glad to hear your red blood's flowing at
last.'

'Pull your head in, Gabe. I'm not planning to make a
pass at her. In fact,' he added, raising his voice for em-
phasis, 'I'm planning to show her that there's nothing
romantic about life with a cattleman.'

Gabe chuckled again. 'All I can say is, don't let her
near Piper. My wife might shoot your argument down
in flames.'

Camille was talking to Megs the cat when Jonno
prowled back through the house to the veranda. Her head
was bent forward as she scratched the ginger tabby
gently between the ears and her dark hair fell in a tumble
of curls that caught fiery-red lights from the setting sun.

At the sound of his footsteps she looked up, her dark
eyes shining, and he felt a startling jolt of desire.

Hell! Every time he saw her he was caught afresh by
how unexpectedly lovely she was.

And *his* reactions weren't his only problem. Camille
was acting as if everything about his place was fascinating and fun. She was supposed to be looking for gritty
realism. How the hell could he impress on her that life
on the land was hard for a woman, that it wasn't the
slightest bit romantic, when she was determined to be
delighted by everything?

From the minute they'd left her hire car at a garage
in Mullinjim and she'd driven home with him in his
truck, she'd carried on a treat about the countryside—
the rolling pastures, the wide skies and the distant hills.

As for the wildlife, every kangaroo, emu, or plains turkey excited her.

'Now that I'm not having to risk my neck in the driver's seat, I can appreciate all this,' she'd said in an attempt to justify her enthusiasm.

The problem was, her delight wasn't over-the-top or insincere. It seemed to be genuine and spontaneous and that bothered Jonno, but he was hanged if he knew why.

Right now she was becoming best friends with his cat.

'She's gorgeous,' she said, running an elegant hand along Megs's spine. 'I've never had a pet.'

'Not even when you were a kid?'

'No. And now we have pet-police running my apartment block and they won't let me have anything, not even a goldfish.'

He resisted the urge to ask why she hadn't had a pet as a child. Getting to know her life history wasn't part of his game plan. She was here on business.

'You're comfortable there, so you stay where you are,' he said gruffly. 'I'm going to get a yard ready for the steers.' He headed for the steps.

'Don't go without me.' She lifted the purring cat from her lap and leapt to her feet. 'I want to experience as much as I can.'

Her face was glowing and he looked away and glared at the low blaze of sunlight on the horizon. He sighed. 'Let's go, then.'

Edenvale's homestead and stock yards had been built on a rise and from here they had a view right down Mullinjim Valley. The grey clouds that had threatened more rain this morning were transformed now, under-lit by pink and gold from the setting sun, and the whole landscape was tinged with a bronzed glow.

At the bottom of the slope lay the billabong, home to various wild ducks and geese, and beyond that stretched long, rolling, grassy paddocks, pale yellow and dotted with clumps of trees and cattle. On the far horizon a low line of purple-pink hills sprawled.

'It's so beautiful here,' Camille said yet again.

Jonno scowled and strode faster, so that she had to almost run to keep up. At the barn, he pulled three bales free from the haystack. 'Can you carry one of these?'

'Sure.' She held out willing arms to take it. 'So what happens now?'

'We spread this in the yard so the calves will have something to eat when they get here. They won't have been fed at the sale yards and, as they're coming off their mothers' milk, we don't want them to lose too much condition.'

As they broke up the bales and laid the hay around the stockyard's fence line, she asked, 'Why don't we spread it all over the pen?'

'It's a waste of time putting hay in the middle—the cattle will only trample it into the mud.'

'That makes sense,' she said, standing with her hands on her hips and admiring their handiwork.

Jonno frowned. 'It's only a stock yard, Camille. Not a work of art.'

Things went from bad to worse when she insisted on cooking their dinner.

'I'm handy in the kitchen,' she said. 'And you must be sick of having to cook for yourself.'

'Actually, I cook a mean steak,' he muttered. 'And I have a cleaning woman who makes a big casserole each week. That lasts me for several days.'

'But you'd like a change, wouldn't you?' she insisted. 'And there's something about being out in the country with animals and hay and gum trees and sunsets that brings out my domesticated instincts.'

He must have looked thoroughly alarmed because she rushed to add, 'Don't worry, Jonno. I only get very occasional doses of domestication. I'm not dangerous. I don't step up to a stove and immediately have visions of a slim gold band and a trip to the altar. Cooking is as far as I go.'

'Glad to know I'm safe,' he said with a wry grin. If only he could be as casual about this as she was. But somehow, letting Camille Devereaux into his kitchen felt more dangerous than entering a bull ride at a rodeo.

Rummaging around in Jonno's kitchen and concocting a meal from what she found was fun. Thinly sliced beef, onions, capsicum, carrot and celery combined with a sweet chilli sauce quickly became a tasty Asian-style stir-fry, but when they sat down to eat at the round pine table, Camille's sense of fun turned edgy.

What was she doing here, alone and sharing an unnatural cosiness with this puzzling, gorgeous man? She'd spent the best part of the day at war with him and yet here they were—just the two of them in his whopping great empty homestead, with a meal to share and a long night ahead.

With Jonno's self-conscious glances and her scream-ing hormones!

They ate in conspicuous, restless silence. Camille would have liked to interview Jonno but suddenly the usual getting-to-know-you type questions made the meal feel too much like a date. Heaven forbid. Jonno was so touchy about husband-hunting women. Any sign that she was attracted to him and he would have her out on her ear and she'd miss out on her story.

And even if he wasn't so hostile, what the heck was the point of being attracted to Jonno Rivers anyhow? They belonged in different worlds.

But she'd never felt so much chemistry. The kitchen was sizzling with it. And a dark, secretive fire burned in Jonno's eyes whenever he looked at her. She'd never been so tongue-tied, so out of her depth...

It was a relief when his chair scraped on the timber floor and he jumped to his feet. 'I can hear the cattle truck bringing your steers.'

He crossed quickly to the row of hooks near the back door where his heavy outdoor coat was hanging. 'You don't have to come outside now. It's cold and you won't be able to see much in the dark.'

'Don't even think about leaving me behind,' Camille cried. 'I have to watch my babies arrive. Just wait while I grab a warm coat from my room.'

Outside it was very cold and very dark. Clouds hid the moon and the lights of the huge cattle truck blazed as bright as meteors as it reversed slowly along the dirt track to the stock yards. Camille couldn't help but ad-mire the driver's skill as he backed his huge double-decker vehicle in line with the relatively narrow loading ramp.

'Just wait here,' Jonno told her. 'We don't want to spook the cattle in the dark. If one falls, we could have a beast with a broken leg.'

She was happy enough to wait in the shadows while he went to speak to the driver. The truck's lights were dimmed and as Jonno had predicted, there was little to see, but she could hear soft snorts and the occasional lowing from the cattle as they stood patiently in the truck, then the loud, grating clang of the big doors opening and a man's voice calling, 'Shoo, shoo!' And finally the clatter of hooves on metal.

By the faint light of the men's torches she saw the first shadowy shapes of the cattle moving down the ramp. One, two, three, four… Her cattle. *Her* cattle. She felt a strange, almost motherly pride in them as they trotted quietly out of the truck like obedient schoolchildren.

She even found herself thinking up names for them… Roland, Seamus, Bruno, Fred, Joe, Lance, Alonzo…

The men only spoke when necessary, keeping their voices low, and she remembered that Jonno had wanted to keep the calves calm. They needed gentle handling…

In the past, her picture of cattlemen had been vague images of sun-drenched, noisy stockmen on horseback, with jingling spurs and cracking stock whips. Not men who stayed up on a cold night to make sure a strange woman's calves settled in without undue stress.

She couldn't help wondering how Jonno Rivers handled a woman he cared about.

* * *

Laughter woke her next morning; the raucous cackles of kookaburras in the gum tree outside her window. Camille lay in bed, squinting through eyelids unwilling to open at this ungodly hour, and saw the pearly light of dawn filtering through white timber shutters.

She closed her eyes again and lay very still, listening to the birds as they laughed riotously. Their guffaws built into a crescendo, then tapered off, only to start up again with another outburst. It was hard not to smile. They sounded so full of energy, so unique, so Australian, so much a part of the outback. She'd never heard a kookaburra in Kings Cross.

And suddenly, out of the blue, she was remembering another time when she'd lain in a bed in a country homestead and woken to laughter. Good grief! She'd forgotten all about that holiday, when she'd spent a summer break at the home of a friend from boarding-school.

Anne Page had lived on a sheep farm on the New England Tableland and Camille could remember lying in the Page family's guest bedroom, listening to the unfamiliar sounds of morning laughter.

Anne and her parents and brother had already got up and gathered in the kitchen for breakfast, and they were all laughing. Proper, unforced, happy laughter.

Tears had streamed down Camille's cheeks. She'd never heard her own parents laughing like that. They'd never had time to share meals, let alone jokes and fun.

And now, years later, as she lay in the back bedroom at Edenvale, Camille tried again to remember a time in her childhood when she'd laughed with her parents. Her father had used to take her to the movies on Saturday afternoons and they'd eaten choc-top ice-cream cones and laughed at the cartoons.

But surely they'd laughed more often than that?

She couldn't remember much laughter. All she could remember were the arguments and the fights. When she saw her father again she would have to ask him. There must have been good times.

There must have been.

Jonno was finishing his breakfast when Camille came into the kitchen, dressed in jeans and ready for action. He wasn't particularly cheered by the fact that she looked as good in the mornings as she did in the middle of the day. Or at night.

Which meant today wasn't going to be any easier than yesterday.

'Have you been up long?' she asked as she helped herself to tea from the big brown pot.

'I've been over to the yards to give the calves some water.'

'I suppose you're always up at the crack of dawn.'

He nodded and looked away abruptly. After he'd spent the night lying wide awake, going crazy with inappropriately lustful thoughts, it had been a relief to see dawn break.

'So what happens now?' Camille asked as she dropped a slice of bread into the toaster. 'What else do you have to do to settle the calves into their new home?'

'Today they'll have to be branded,' he said.

Her head snapped up. 'Branded?'

'Yeah. I have to brand, ear-tag, vaccinate and dip them. Then tomorrow I'll take them down the run to another yard close by. I'll keep them fed on hay for a few days. It's important to keep them as calm as possible. Then I might practise herding them in the road just to get them used to being rounded up. After that I'll take them out to a more distant paddock.'

'I had no idea my boys would take up so much of your time. I guess you had other work planned,' she said.

Jonno almost made a sarcastic quip about putting his feet up, but thought better of it.

'Do you *have* to brand them?' Camille asked.

'It's the only way we have legal proof of ownership.'

'I suppose…but I thought you wanted to avoid stressing them. Branding seems so brutal.' She sighed. 'Poor Alonzo.'

'Alonzo?'

Her cheeks turned pink. 'Never mind. Slip of the tongue.' Her toast was done and she lifted it onto a plate. 'I suppose worrying about branding is the kind of soft and soppy thing you'd expect from a city girl like me.'

'You don't have to watch.' He would be a hell of a lot happier if she didn't watch. 'Listen,' he said, 'I don't think this is going to work—having you here. It would have been better if you kept going yesterday. Why don't you head off this morning?'

'No,' she cried. 'Don't get me wrong about the branding. I didn't mean to be critical. I want to experience everything. I don't want a watered-down version of realism. I need hands-on experience.'

'One thing I can promise you *won't* get here is hands-on experience,' he growled.

'Why not?'

For painful seconds their eyes met across the kitchen table and Jonno's words seemed to take on overwhelming significance. *One thing I can promise is you* won't *get hands-on experience.*

It was probably the stupid after effects of his crazy, restless night, but he sensed a shock of unwelcome awareness again and saw that same shock mirrored in Camille's eyes—as if they'd both reached out and caressed each other intimately.

Bull's balls!

Jumping to his feet, he crossed quickly to rinse his mug at the sink. 'I can't let someone as inexperienced as you get close to the cattle,' he said. 'Stock work's hard and it can be dangerous. I can't risk getting you hurt.'

'But they're my cattle,' she said. 'And in the interests of accuracy I need to get up close and personal with them.'

'And, in the interests of avoiding a lawsuit from *Girl Talk* magazine, I intend to save your delicate neck.' He headed for the door. 'Take your time over breakfast,' he called without looking back at her. 'Come down to the yard if you must. But be prepared to keep out of the way.'

Despite her bold claims at breakfast Camille flinched inwardly as she headed for the stock yard. She knew she would hate what was about to happen.

'Stay here and keep your distance,' Jonno ordered, pointing to a spot next to a metal contraption that looked like some modern version of a mediaeval torture rack.

'What's that?' she asked.

'It's the crush. We use it to control the cattle while we work on them.'

The crush. How apt. Something from the Spanish Inquisition. Why not the rack as well?

She glanced to her left and saw a roaring blue flame from a gas bottle playing onto a large branding iron that glowed cherry-red with heat, and she felt her insides churn.

Just remember this is realism. It's all part of the story.

To her right she saw Jonno sending the first of her cattle along a narrow passageway formed by two lines of high steel fencing.

Her poor boys. She couldn't resist hurrying forward to offer a soothing word.

'Don't stand in front of him or he'll balk,' Jonno growled. 'I thought I told you to stay put.'

He shoved her aside and spread his long arms wide, operating a lever with one hand while he used the other to skilfully push the steer into the confines of the crush.

As Camille watched, he pulled another lever and an opening appeared at the other end. The poor animal quickly tried to get through, but there was another swift movement from Jonno and the steer was held firmly between the closing metal jaws of the crush.

Camille clasped her hands to her mouth in horror. 'Oh, the poor thing, it's helpless.'

'That's what this whole process is about. Now, stand

back, will you, while I drench and ear-tag this little guy?'

He used a pistol-like dispenser to squirt a small amount of liquid down the animal's back. 'Used to have to plunge them through a dip in the old days, now it's just a quick spray to keep them free from ticks.'

With the easy, fluid actions of an athlete, he moved quickly back and forth between his work bench and the crush, picking up a plastic bag of vaccine with a tube and syringe attached and giving the beast its protective jab, then back to the bench to hang the bag on a nail.

Within seconds he'd moved to the front of the crush and there was a short bellow from the steer as he attached a plastic tag to its ear with an ugly-looking stapler.

'Does it hurt?' Camille called.

He grinned back at her. 'Probably as much as you were hurt when someone tagged you with those little gold earrings.'

And then the red-hot branding iron was in his hands. Swiftly and precisely, he applied it to the steer's shoulder. There was a short bellow of complaint from the animal and the smell of burning hair.

Camille clamped her hand over her mouth to hold back her protest and watched as Jonno flipped another lever and the beast trotted out of the open jaws of the crush.

'That must have been absolutely terrifying for him,' she said as Jonno returned the branding iron to the flame. 'Can't someone come up with a better way of doing it?'

His face was stony as he pushed past her and went to

fetch the next calf. 'As they say, if you can't stand the heat...stay out of the kitchen.'

'There's no need to be a monster!'

For a moment he tensed, then he turned back to her. 'You might think I'm a monster but have a look at your little...Alonzo.'

He pointed behind her and Camille turned to see the animal with its head down, chomping into some of the lucerne hay only a few yards from where it had been released from its torment. With big brown eyes it stared at them and chewed contentedly, strings of lucerne hanging from its mouth.

'They've got thick hides,' he said. 'I don't think he's going to need first aid or counselling, do you?'

She found herself nodding her agreement. She had to admit the calf didn't *look* to be in ongoing pain. 'Maybe not.'

Jonno went to work on the next steer and Camille found herself becoming more fascinated than horrified. She edged closer, unable to keep her eyes off the neat fit of Jonno's faded jeans and the hard-packed muscles rippling in his shoulders and arms as he worked. The colour photo of him that they'd published in *Girl Talk* had hinted at his lean, leashed strength, but to see it in action was something else.

What would it be like to have that fit, toned body and all that restrained energy concentrated on her? Surely Jonno Rivers would be a sensational lover.

For crying out loud! Where had that thought come from? How could one man plus sweat and dust and cattle add up to so much sex appeal?

What was happening to her? Most girls swooned when there was jasmine scent in the air, red wine on the table and a gypsy violinist in the background. And here she was, feeling steamy when there was nothing but dusty yards, a branding iron and a mob of cattle.

And what was the matter with Jonno? He was standing stock-still and staring at her, drench gun in hand, wearing a bewildered expression she was sure matched her own.

'Are you planning to free me of ticks as well?' she asked, pointing with a breathless little laugh to the gun.

'Sorry,' he muttered, a red flush staining his neck. 'I was distracted.'

This was ridiculous. She had to stop thinking amorous thoughts about this man. 'Look,' she said, pointing to the cattle race. 'I know how you do all this now, so you should let me help.'

He scowled. 'No way.'

'But you have to do about a dozen things at once. Come on, give me one tiny task.'

He didn't answer but gave an annoyed shake of his head.

'Wouldn't you normally have help with this?'

'There are only fifteen of them. It's a small job,' he muttered with a shrug.

'But surely an extra hand, even from a city girl, is better than no help at all.'

From the pocket of her jeans, she pulled a piece of paper. 'I've written you a disclaimer, Jonno, freeing you from any legal ramifications if I get hurt.' She took two steps towards him and thrust the paper into his hand. 'I meant it yesterday when I said I'm a damn good journalist. And I've put my job on the line to give you your freedom. You owe me this chance.'

She watched the rise and fall of his shoulders and chest and the frowning furrow between his brows as he scanned her note. 'I bet you normally have someone sending those calves down the race for you,' she prompted.

He lifted his gaze from the paper and his crooked smile was slow in coming, but when it did it sent heat flashing under her skin.

'OK,' he said. 'You'd better have a go. At least these little fellows are only half-grown. They can't do too much damage.'

He showed her how to approach a steer from the side, so that it separated from the mob and hurried away from her, and he gave her a long piece of plastic pipe to tap it on the back if necessary. He made it look easy, of course.

'Make sure you're always behind the cattle and never in front of them,' he said. Then he walked back to the crush and, after sending her a wave and an encouraging grin, he called, 'OK. You can send one down the race.'

And, of course, that was when her heart began to thump and her stomach tightened and she wondered why on earth she'd ever opened her big mouth. Did she really want to do this?

She took a minuscule step towards the nearest steer. It was rather a pretty fellow with a white face and a curly red coat. 'Go on,' she urged it softly.

It didn't budge.

'Go on,' she tried, more loudly.

It turned and stared at her with big brown eyes. 'Jonno won't you hurt very much,' she said.

'Get in a bit closer,' called Jonno.

Oh, crumbs! She took another step and made a shooing gesture. The steer lurched away towards the gate, exactly where she wanted him to go. 'That's it, keep going,' she called, moving behind it. It ran through the open gate into the narrow race lined with tall fences.

'Got it,' he cried. 'Good on you!'

With one eye on the rest of the mob in the pen, she watched Jonno move with impressive speed to vaccinate, ear-tag and brand. She was still staring in admiration when he called, 'Next!' And she realised she should have had another steer ready and waiting.

But by the time they'd processed another eight animals, she was starting to get into the swing of things. She had worked out how to approach them so that they would move forward immediately.

'You're doing well,' Jonno called. 'You're a natural.'

Her heart gave a queer little jump and she felt as ridiculously proud as a first-grader who'd been given a smiley stamp for printing her name neatly.

This task was so different from anything she'd ever done before and yet it was strangely satisfying. She enjoyed the physical activity and the sense of timing involved. And she felt a ridiculously warm glow at the thought that her 'boys' now belonged officially on Edenvale.

They wore the Edenvale brand, the letter E over inverted wings, and she felt a sense of connection that wasn't exactly warranted, but made her inexplicably happy.

'The last ones are often a bit frisky!' Jonno called. 'If you like, you can send them down together.'

'OK,' she called back and shooed the final two calves towards the race. They jumped and head butted each other a little, but once they entered the race they trotted forward quietly.

Camille drew a deep, satisfied breath and dropped her gaze to her ruined boots. The experience had been worth wrecking her best boots in all this mud.

'Shut the gate!' yelled Jonno.

Glancing up, she saw that the last calf, which was slightly smaller than the others, had managed to turn in the race and was charging back towards her.

She darted forward and reached for the gate, ready to slam it.

Wham!

A massive thump propelled her backwards and the ground leapt up and punched the breath out of her lungs.

'Camille!'

The branding iron clattered on the concrete floor as Jonno saw her fall. His heart vaulted into his throat as he raced towards her.

She was lying very still.

Hell! How badly was she hurt? When the last steer had turned back, it had sent the partly opened gate slamming into her. He rushed into the yard and sank to his knees beside her. 'Camille!'

Why wasn't she moving? A cold, hard ball of fear tightened in his stomach. He touched her shoulder and her hand moved as if she was trying to communicate. Thank God she was conscious.

'Are you OK?' he asked her. 'Where are you hurt?'

Her eyes opened, she swore, then muttered, 'I—I think I'm OK.'

From head to toe she was covered in mud and pieces of straw, and there was blood on her chin where the gate had clipped her.

Between gasps for breath, she cursed again.

'Are you sure you're OK? Do your ribs hurt?'

'I just got an almighty shock,' she grunted. 'Where did he come from?'

'Here, let me help you to sit up.'

'Yeah, thanks.'

As he crouched beside her she sagged back against his thigh and he was relieved to see that, apart from the blood on her chin, she didn't seem to be carrying any injuries. He did his best to ignore the warm weight of her resting against the inside of his leg by reproaching himself for putting her in a position where this could happen.

'Oh, yuck!' Camille groaned as she touched a hand to her chin and saw blood on her fingers. She hated the sight of blood, especially her own.

Jonno leaned closer, his gaze concentrated as he examined her chin with a gentle touch. 'I think it's only a graze,' he said. 'Are you sore anywhere else? Did that gate hurt you?'

'I don't think so. It took me by surprise. I'm sorry, I forgot to shut it properly.'

She looked into his eyes. They were only inches away

and full of concern. For her. Oh, man! Here she was, melting in the cradle of Jonno Rivers's strong thighs with his gorgeous, sexy mouth poised just above hers. What a moment to be covered in mud and blood!

'I'll take you back to the house,' he said.

'I think I can walk. I was winded a little, but I'm OK now.' What a pity she was primed to be honest. She was dying for him to pick her up. Heavens, she was dim. Why hadn't she pretended to be more hurt than she was?

'Don't move! I'll carry you.'

Oh, yes! Before she could make a feeble attempt to argue, he slipped a hand beneath her knees and another around her shoulders and lifted her effortlessly.

'Jonno, it's a long way to the house. You can't take me all that way.' *Shut up, Camille. Let him do it.*

He didn't speak and Camille sighed dramatically as she looped an arm around his neck. What else was a girl to do? Most of the time she was a feminist, but if a seriously handsome man was absolutely determined to rescue her she might as well give herself up to the heady experience of being carried in strong, muscular arms as if she weighed no more than a kitten or a bag of groceries.

All in all it was incredibly flattering.

If the girls in the office could see me now they'd be as green as beans!

In the kitchen he settled her onto a chair and ordered her not to move while he fetched towels, a basin of warm water and a bottle of disinfectant.

As he soaked a face cloth in the basin of water and disinfectant then squeezed the excess moisture out again,

Camille watched his hands. They were tanned and as nicely shaped as the rest of him, with a smattering of sun-bleached hair on the backs and long, strong fingers.

'Hold still while I get the mud off your face so we can see what damage has been done.'

'Mud packs are supposed to be good for the complexion,' she said, hoping to lighten the situation. He was looking far too serious and anxious.

He smiled faintly. 'So you'd like me to leave all this muck on, would you?'

'Er—maybe not. I just remembered the cow pats in that stock yard.'

She was grateful that he didn't allow his gaze to lock with hers as he worked from her forehead down, wiping away the mud. It would be a shade embarrassing if he realised how much she was enjoying his attentions.

When he got to her chin he used a fresh cloth and fresh water and disinfectant and worked very gently, but she couldn't help flinching.

'When I get this cleaned up, we should ice it so you don't bruise.'

'It's not much more than a scratch, is it?'

'I don't think it will leave a lasting scar.' He used the over-casual voice people adopted when they wanted to hide their anxiety.

'Jonno,' she said, 'please don't worry. I promised I'm not going to sue you. I'm sure I haven't been disfigured and, anyway, I did insist on being involved.'

She tried for another joke. 'If only those dozens of poor women who wanted to marry you had known they simply had to fall over to get you down on one knee.'

Again he didn't respond as he knelt beside her and dabbed carefully at her chin, his expression super-concentrated as he made sure it was clean. And at some point during the process Camille stopped wanting to make jokes. But she couldn't stop staring at Jonno.

There was a flushed intensity about his face and his throat worked as if he was feeling...nervous or un-easy...and when he patted her face dry with a soft towel, his movements became slower and slower...even more tender.

His eyes were focused on her mouth.

And her mind flashed up a crazy picture of Jonno washing her all over. Jonno trickling warm water over her naked thighs...and his hands...

She felt so suddenly tight she could hardly breathe. Her insides were coiling taut with longing. A heavy heat sank low in her stomach and her limbs turned languorous and boneless.

Jonno's eyes flashed up to meet hers and she *knew* he was feeling as helpless and trapped as she was, com-pelled by an impossible, unwise yearning. Something be-yond their control.

He didn't speak, but his eyes burned deep into hers. She lowered her gaze to his mouth. Those sensuous lips were designed to drive a woman's common sense to kingdom come. Jonno this close was temptation plus!

Her imagination raced ahead and she could already feel his mouth taking hers, and the thought of those lips on her skin filled her head like a billowing, spreading cloud of steam.

'Camille,' he whispered.

With a rush of sweet warmth, she saw that he'd dropped the towel and was settling his hands on the wooden seat of the chair on either side of her.

And he was leaning towards her.

CHAPTER FOUR

ONLY their mouths touched.

Jonno didn't hold her. He kept his hands on the chair and was careful not to bump her chin as he brushed his lips over hers, moving slowly back and forth in a teasing whisper of gentle sensations.

She'd never known such an exquisite, melting moment. Straight from her dreams.

'I'll hurt your chin,' he murmured in a throaty whisper against her mouth.

'You couldn't,' she whispered back. She was already on fire; she would be immune to pain. How could a simple, hardly there kiss make her feel this way?

Slowly, slowly Jonno increased the pressure of his mouth on hers, slanting the angle so he didn't hurt her chin. He tasted the corner of her mouth, kissed the little mole above her upper lip and gently, lazily, drew her lower lip between his and sucked.

Only her muddy clothes prevented her from flinging her arms around his neck and hauling him closer, but she grabbed handfuls of his shirt, and her eyes drifted closed as he teased the seam of her lips with his tongue. Her mouth opened. She was trembling on the knife-edge of shattering passion, inviting him to seek and taste and explore her as intimately as he wished. His kiss became hard, demanding deeper access. She heard desire rumble like a roll of thunder deep in his throat.

And footsteps.

'Oh, heavens! I should have knocked.'

Jonno's head jerked away from her as a voice sounded in the doorway. Over his shoulder, Camille saw a slim blonde woman standing in the kitchen doorway with a plump baby boy in her arms and a wide-eyed little girl at her side.

'Piper!' Jonno cried, jumping to his feet, and Camille felt ridiculously guilty, as if she'd been caught shoplifting.

'Sorry,' the woman said, her blue eyes expressing embarrassment mixed with curiosity. 'I didn't think to knock; I just barged in.'

A dark flush stained Jonno's face as he stooped to pick up the bowl and discarded towels. 'We had a slight accident in the yard. A steer knocked Camille flat.'

'Did he kick you?' the woman asked, the sparkle in her gaze dimming when she saw Camille's chin.

'No. Actually, I'm fine.' Camille got to her feet, hoping she would feel less flustered if she was standing. 'I'm covered in mud, but otherwise I'm fine.'

'Let me introduce you,' Jonno said quickly. 'Camille Devereaux, this is my sister-in-law, Piper Rivers.'

The two women exchanged cautious smiles. Dressed in a pale pink blouse and slim blue jeans, Piper had a sunny expression and a glowing, outdoorsy look. To Camille, she seemed incredibly young and slim to be the mother of the cute little girl and the bouncing baby boy with the chubby face and toothless grin.

Camille guessed that she was probably around her own age—twenty-seven.

'These scallywags are my niece, Bella, and my nephew, Michael.'

'Hi, guys,' Camille said, waving. She hadn't had much experience with children.

'I think you've already met Piper's husband, Gabe,' Jonno added.

'Oh, yes, the helicopter man. I met him in Mullinjim yesterday.' Camille held out a hand to Piper and then pulled it back sharply. 'Goodness, I can't shake hands. I'm too dirty. I was just about to have a shower.'

'I'm very pleased to meet you, Camille,' Piper said with a warm, wide smile, and Camille couldn't help liking her.

The little girl tugged at Jonno's jeans. 'Is this lady going to help you to babysit us, Uncle Jonno?'

'Ah…' Jonno looked momentarily stunned.

'You did remember you volunteered to babysit, didn't you, Jonno?' Piper asked, frowning. 'Gabe and I are going to the Cattlemen's Association Annual Dinner in Mount Isa.'

'Oh, yes, of course! I hadn't really forgotten—I was just momentarily sidetracked. Camille bought some steers yesterday.' As if to cover his embarrassment, he bent down hurriedly and scooped up Bella with one hand while he tickled her with the other. The little girl wriggled and squealed with delight.

'Are you sure it's still OK to leave them with you?' Piper asked, addressing her query more towards Camille than to Jonno.

'Good heavens, yes,' cried Camille. 'Please don't change any plans because of me. I'm here simply as an observer. I'm a journalist and Jonno is—is helping me to—um—to observe all aspects of outback life. In the yards, in the paddock...' Embarrassment always made her ramble and she was feeling seriously embarrassed right now. 'If babysitting is part of the picture, it adds an interesting human dimension.'

Her gaze linked briefly with Jonno's and then she made her excuses and hurried away to the bathroom, blushing as she wondered what he was thinking of the very human dimension they'd recently added to their strictly business relationship.

When she came into the kitchen after her shower, baby Michael was sitting on the floor, blissfully banging two saucepan lids together, and Piper was sitting alone at the table.

'Jonno's taken Bella down to the billabong to see the ducks,' she said.

A teapot, two mugs, a milk jug and sugar bowl had been set on the table and Camille guessed that a cosy chat was planned. Would Piper expect her to explain why she'd been kissing the living daylights out of her brother-in-law after an acquaintance of less than twenty-four hours?

'How's the chin now?' Piper asked.

'It's fine, just a graze,' said Camille.

'Would you like some tea?'

Camille took a seat and bit back an urge to ask for coffee. She'd been drinking too much coffee. 'Thanks.'

'I'm relieved you weren't badly hurt,' Piper said as she poured the tea, then her face pulled into a wry grin. 'But I have to admit I was a little worried when Gabe told me there was a journalist from *Girl Talk* staying here. I had visions of a full-scale war erupting.'

Camille smiled as she accepted the mug. 'There were one or two moments yesterday when I was tempted to punch Jonno on the nose.' She shrugged. 'But he's too big and, well, we seem to have managed a—a temporary truce.'

Piper lifted her mug in a smiling salute. 'I always say you can't beat a good truce.'

Camille knew she was referring to the interrupted kiss.

As if she'd been embarrassed by her own forwardness, Piper blushed and bent down quickly to move a saucepan lid closer to her baby son, but when she looked Camille's way again she said, 'While we're on our own, I thought perhaps we could have a little—' a faint smile tugged at her lips and she shrugged '—girl talk.'

'If you like,' Camille said cautiously.

'Gabe suggested that I should explain—about why Jonno's been so…so uncooperative with your magazine.'

Camille's breath caught on a surprised gasp. 'I'd appreciate that.' She leaned closer. 'I couldn't get anything out of Jonno, except that he didn't want to be involved in the project in the first place.'

'It's that stubborn Rivers pride,' Piper said. 'I've known the Rivers men all my life. I grew up next door to them and they're proud and tough on the outside, but big softies at heart. Jonno's really taken an emotional beating over your project.'

'I—I'm sorry to hear that.'

'I'm sure your magazine was motivated by good intentions, but the results have been embarrassing. Jonno could probably have coped with a deluge of mail, but there have been so many women turning up on Edenvale's doorstep uninvited: women looking for his financial help, or wanting to mother him, cook for him, sleep with him. They've been chasing after him any way they could. And, of course, he's had to cope with all kinds of stupid, humorous remarks from some of the local community as well.'

Camille remembered the teasing grins and taunts at the sale yards yesterday.

'But I don't understand how he became involved against his will,' said Camille. 'Did someone forge his entry?'

'Yes,' said Piper. 'He was framed.' The baby on the floor began to fuss and she picked him up, kissed him and settled him on her lap. 'I'm going to have to feed this little tiger in a moment and then get ready. Gabe will be here soon.'

'But you must tell me quickly who did this to Jonno. Off the record, of course.'

Piper glanced quickly towards the door and lowered her voice. 'Jonno's former girlfriend, Suzanne Heath, sent in the entry. She sent you an old photo that she'd kept and she forged his signature.'

'For heaven's sake, why? Was it revenge for being dumped?'

Piper pursed her lips. 'Actually, Suzanne was the dumper and Jonno was the dumpee. She and Jonno had a traumatic, on-again-off-again relationship until Suzanne's true colours showed.' She let out a noisy sigh and hugged her baby boy closer. 'Suzanne became pregnant and Jonno wanted to marry her. It was quite incredible how excited he was when he thought he was going to be a dad.'

'Really?' Camille's throat felt choked with unexpected emotion.

'Yes. So it was just awful when he found out that the baby wasn't his. Suzanne had been seeing another fellow, Charles Kilgour, as well.'

'Poor Jonno.' Camille felt such a strong pang of sympathy that her eyes stung and her throat hurt. 'But that doesn't explain why this Suzanne woman sent Jonno's name in to *Girl Talk*.'

Shaking her head, Piper gave an exasperated roll of her eyes. 'She doesn't live around here any more, or I would have tackled her about that. But apparently she claims she was trying to make it up to Jonno by fixing him up with another girlfriend.' Her eyebrows rose. 'That shows you how dense the woman is.'

'Indeed.'

'As if Jonno Rivers couldn't catch any woman he wanted without the help of an old flame.'

'Exactly,' replied Camille, keeping her eyes discreetly downcast as she realised that Piper was probably thinking she wanted Jonno, too. 'The girls in my office all wanted him for themselves,' she added quickly. 'In fact *they* would find it hard to believe that this Suzanne woman turned him down.'

Piper looked faintly amused. 'Yes, I suppose *they* would.' She shook her head. 'But Suzanne is a party animal. She didn't take the cattle business as seriously as Jonno and got bored with his dedication to the property. To be honest, she and Charles Kilgour deserve each other.'

'I see.' Camille chewed her lower lip thoughtfully. 'Is Jonno still carrying a torch for her?'

Piper laughed. 'After what she's done to him? You've got to be joking.' She cast a more speculative glance Camille's way. 'So this truce of yours…' She hesitated.

'I'd already agreed to drop Jonno from the project—even before you told me this.'

'Great. That's a relief.'

'I'm putting together a piece on life in the outback instead—from a city girl's perspective.'

Piper grinned. 'Feel free to come over to Windaroo after we get home tomorrow. I'd be happy to show you life in the outback—from a country girl's perspective of course.' Baby Michael grizzled and nuzzled at her chest. 'But right now this outback woman had better go and get her son and heir fed and settled,' she said. 'Fingers crossed, he should have a nice, long nap this afternoon and then all you'll have to deal with is Bella. I'm afraid that little madam is a handful, but luckily she adores Jonno.'

Jonno saw Camille coming down the slope to the billabong where he was helping Bella catch tadpoles in a jam jar. His eyes followed her progress, glancing back to make sure Bella was safe as she danced at the water's edge, and then back to Camille.

In her slim-fitting blue jeans and dark red shirt and with his dog, Saxon, bounding beside her, Camille made a charming picture. Her dark chocolate curls bounced as she moved with the slender grace of a dancer, bending one moment to pat Saxon and rub his ears and then straightening and arching her neck to watch the flight of a flock of wood ducks.

When she reached him her eyes glowed and her lips parted in a slow smile of greeting, and all he could think about was kissing her again...which was pretty bloody stupid.

'I've caught seven tadpoles,' announced Bella, who had a habit of ignoring normal methods of greeting. She thrust her jar towards Camille.

'Seven? How about that?' Camille crouched low and inspected the little black bodies suspended in the water. 'They're cute little fat guys, aren't they? What are you going to do with them?'

'I'll take them home and put them in our creek.'

Camille nodded. 'A little crossbreeding will probably be good for the species.'

Bella looked puzzled. 'What does that mean?'

Camille shot Jonno a helpless glance. 'It means I don't know how to talk to children.'

'Don't worry,' he laughed. 'Bella will conduct a running commentary on any topic.'

Soon Bella set her tadpoles aside and began to play with Saxon. 'Tell me about Piper,' Camille said to him.

'I'm intrigued by her. I'm sure she would be great material for my article.'

He studied her for a thoughtful moment. 'What sorts of things do you want to know?'

'What's her life like? How does she spend her days? Is she involved in running Windaroo?'

'Too right! There isn't a thing Piper doesn't know about cattle and running a property. She has some help from Gabe, of course, but his main interest is his helicopter business. Piper musters with the men, works as hard as anyone else in the yards, keeps the station books, plans the breeding schedule...'

'And she balances all that with her role as a wife and mother of two?'

'Yes.' His eyes were speculative as they met hers. 'The problem is Piper makes her demanding life look impossibly easy.'

'Women in the city can do that, too,' she told him, frowning.

Jonno shrugged and glanced up towards the homestead. 'Take a look at her now.'

Piper waved to them from the veranda. She'd showered and changed into a glamorous blue silk gown and her corn-gold hair was flowing freely to her shoulders. Even from this distance Camille could see the sparkle of diamond earrings and the dramatic effects of careful make-up.

'No sign of a cowgirl now,' she admitted. 'So she's a modern-day Cinderella, too.'

'And here comes her prince.'

A throbbing motor chugged overhead and within

minutes a helicopter was landing in the paddock next to the billabong. Fascinated, Camille watched as Gabe Rivers, looking tall, dark and super-handsome in evening clothes, climbed down from the helicopter and Piper hurried down the slope to meet him.

'Oh, if only I had my camera,' she sighed. She watched them come together and saw the way Gabe smiled at his wife. His face glowed with a look of such blinding, naked love that Camille felt the shock of its impact and an embarrassing prickle of tears, as if she'd trespassed on something very private.

She had never known anyone who would look at her like that. Not her parents. No one. In her wildest dreams, she couldn't imagine a man looking at her that way. She'd never even hoped for it…but seeing Piper and Gabe made her wonder if perhaps she should.

'I'm supposed to be writing about the lack of romance in the outback,' she told Jonno, her tone slightly more snappy than she'd meant it to be. 'But that couple seem extremely romantic.'

With Bella in his arms, Jonno was waving to her parents as their helicopter lifted off once more, but he sent Camille a swift, guarded frown. 'Gabe and Piper have something very rare.'

'I guess you're right.' She sighed thoughtfully.

As they stood side by side until the chopper became a speck in the blue distance, the atmosphere around them seemed brittle and tense, as if they were both wondering what the other was thinking.

'If you're really keen to get the full picture of things in the outback, including the less romantic side,' Jonno drawled, 'the fodder troughs need cleaning this afternoon. That would quickly change your rose-coloured views of this place.'

Camille's chin hiked to a haughty angle, and she winced slightly as the sudden movement made her grazed skin sting. How dense of her to be thinking about the way he'd kissed her. It might have been sensational, but he certainly wasn't looking for a repeat performance.

'I'd love to clean your troughs,' she said with as much icy dignity as she could muster, and she hurried towards the yards, feeling a spurt of triumph at the way his jaw had dropped open with surprise.

What the hell was the matter with him?

Jonno couldn't believe how crazily he'd let himself stumble from one foolish mistake to another. First he'd invited Camille Devereaux into his home and, as if that hadn't been stupid enough, he'd lost his head and kissed her. Lost *himself* in the simplest and sweetest of kisses. The lingering taste and feel of her warm, honey-sweet, inviting mouth had been driving him mad all afternoon.

He'd retired to his study to do book work and had kept Bella amused with story books and a computer game, but most of the time he'd watched Camille through the study window as she'd scoured the troughs with an impressive amount of energy—and an impressive *derrière* pointed skywards.

Now this evening he felt guilty that he was letting her cook dinner again. And he'd only put up the weakest resistance.

I shouldn't let her act as if she's at home in my

kitchen. Yeah, right. And he shouldn't be sitting at the kitchen table pretending to read his mail while sneaking long looks at her as she worked at the sink, peeling vegetables. Her dark hair kept parting to reveal the delightfully kissable pale skin of her graceful neck and it took all his will-power to stay in his chair.

'Someone's been sleeping in my bed,' cried a small voice, and Bella stormed into the kitchen, her green eyes flashing.

Blast. He'd forgotten about the bed situation. 'You're right, Goldilocks,' he said, ruffling his niece's blonde curls. 'Camille slept in your bed last night.' Without missing a beat, he added, 'And she will tonight, too.'

'But it's *my* bed,' Bella insisted with a stamp of her foot. 'I always sleep there when you mind me, Uncle Jonno.'

'I know, poppet, but I have lots of beds. I'll fix you another one for tonight. Camille already has her things unpacked in that back bedroom.'

Camille turned from the sink. 'I can easily shift my gear.'

'No.' Jonno shook his head at her and sent her a warning frown. Bella was inclined to be bossy and liked to get her own way and he didn't think it was wise to give in to her. He turned back to Bella. 'How would you like to sleep in a big, bouncy double bed tonight?'

'No!' she cried and her bottom lip stuck out in a stubborn pout. 'I want my little white bed. Camille can sleep in the big bed. She's big.' She frowned at Jonno, then her eyes widened as if a new thought had struck. 'She can sleep in your bed.'

'Ah—no, Bella. That's not a good idea.'

Hell! His blood heated and his body throbbed at the very thought!

Camille kept her back to him and scrubbed fiercely at a potato, but he saw a rosy tide creeping up the back of her neck.

'Why can't she sleep with you?' came Bella's piping voice. 'You're both grow-nuts. You can be like Mummy and Daddy.'

He wondered if Camille was smiling, but she kept her head turned away.

'Your mummy and daddy are married,' he said. 'Only married people sleep in the same bed.' He spoke with his eyes fixed entirely on Camille, who was cutting the eyes out of a potato with the intense concentration of a brain surgeon. 'Isn't that right, Camille?'

He saw her shoulders stiffen before she turned, her eyebrows lifted in high arcs of surprise. 'I'm sure that's the rule in this house.' She looked directly at him and her dark eyes flashed brightly. He couldn't tell if she was angry or amused by the conversation. Then she turned quickly back to the sink and began to attack another potato.

'But I saw you kissing Camille,' Bella insisted. 'That's like being married, isn't it? Daddy's always kissing Mummy.'

Jonno jumped to his feet. 'That's enough talk about kissing.' He scooped the little girl up and tickled her tummy.

'But you *were* kissing.'

'Camille hurt her chin and I had to give her one tiny, get-better kiss. Now, let's go and make up your bed.'

'Let Bella have the little bed,' came Camille's voice as they reached the doorway. 'I'd love to sleep in a big bed tonight.'

Jonno glanced back at her and their gazes locked. Her eyes were dark, luminous and sexy...and *ambiguous*.

'Right,' he said, swallowing. She wasn't talking about his bed. *She wasn't!* 'You win, Bella. You get the little bed and one big bed for Camille coming up.'

'Bella's asleep at last.' Jonno spoke softly as he came into the lamp-lit lounge. 'How's the baby?'

Camille was curled on the sofa, watching a direct telecast of the tennis at Wimbledon with the sound turned down. She gave a little cry of triumph and held up an empty baby's bottle. 'Michael's been fed, burped, changed and rocked back to sleep.'

'Well done!' smiled Jonno. 'I'm impressed. That's quite an achievement. I thought you said you knew nothing about babies.'

'I don't, but he's a little trooper,' she said. 'And the best thing about him is he can't talk. I don't think I could manage Bella with all her questions.'

'She's hard work,' he agreed.

'But you think she's wonderful, don't you?'

His smile deepened. 'I'm nuts about her.'

She felt the cushions move as he flopped onto the far end of the sofa and, glancing sideways, she caught her breath as she saw his sexy masculinity enhanced by the soft glow of the lamp-light. He was wearing a black woollen sweater that emphasised his high, craggy cheek-bones and tousled, crow-black hair.

She forced her eyes back to the white-clad figures on the silent screen.

But all at once the fate of the Australian tennis player at Wimbledon lost her interest. Which was silly! It was madness to let her mind wander into fantasy land just because she was remembering that kiss.

She had to stop thinking about it. Had to keep a tight rein on her mind. But over and over a voice in her head kept prompting: if his simple kiss could make you feel like that, what would it be like to—?

Give it a miss, Camille! Don't let your mind go there! What's the point? You're going back to Sydney.

Uncurling her legs, she arranged herself in a more demure pose, took a deep breath and dredged her thoughts for something safe to talk about. 'Do you baby-sit Bella and Michael very often?'

He met her gaze and smiled slowly. 'Not really. I have Bella here now and again, but most times Piper takes the baby with her, or my parents, who've retired and live in town, look after them. But today it was easier for Gabe to land the chopper here.'

He turned so his body was angled towards her with one denim-clad knee resting on a cushion and a casual arm draped along the back of the sofa. His mouth tilted into a wry smile. 'I guess there won't be much call on you to know about children if you don't plan to marry.'

'I—I guess not.'

Leaning closer, he asked, 'How's the chin?'

'It's fine, thank you. That antiseptic cream is working well.'

He reached out and touched her face gently with the tips of his fingers, but there was nothing gentle about the fierce light in his eyes.

A thrill of anticipation spiralled through her. *Do it!* a wicked voice whispered. *Kiss him. Think of all the women he's turned away. He never gave them this chance. Go for it.*

But another part of her mind was urging her to remember why kissing Jonno Rivers wasn't a good idea. She could only stay here another day at the most and then she would be heading back to Sydney...

Problem was...that argument felt fudgy and old-fashioned and...

He leaned closer and she smelled his aftershave and the soft wool of his sweater. His hand cupped her cheek and his thumb traced a warm line down towards her lips.

Camille leaned into his touch, feeling deliciously warm, sensuous and seduced, and then jackknifed back as an unwelcome thought hit her. Edith! Good grief! She was supposed to call her editor tonight.

At that very moment the telephone rang.

Her heart leapt. Jonno groaned, then straightened and glared in the direction of the strident sound.

'I'll get that,' Camille said, jumping up from the sofa.

But his hand caught her arm. 'Don't worry. I'd better answer it. It's probably Piper ringing to check that everything's OK with the children, but it could be business.'

The nearest phone was in his study and Camille

pressed a nervous hand to her mouth as he crossed the room quickly and disappeared down the hall. What would Jonno think if he had to field a call from her boss?

Her stomach churned.

Too quickly she heard his returning footsteps and when he came into the room his face was dark with anger.

'The call's for you,' he hissed between gritted teeth. 'From Sydney. It's your boss.'

Jumping to her feet, she realised that her knees were distinctly shaky, and as she tried to cross the room Jonno blocked her path.

'She's so pleased I'm staying with "The Bachelor Project".' His voice was hard-edged and his lip curled into a bitter sneer. 'She knew you'd sweet-talk me round.'

'But I told her the deal with you is off.'

'Oh, yeah? Well, she didn't get the message.'

'That's Edith,' Camille said, rolling her eyes. 'Jonno, please don't be mad. I can explain. I—'

'Don't bother. Just get in there and explain *again* to your boss that I'm through with your magazine.'

'Yes, of course, but Jonno, please—'

'She's waiting,' he snarled. 'And she doesn't sound the patient type.'

Jonno prowled through the house to the kitchen, not bothering to turn on the light. He stood at the sink in the unheated, darkened room, and looked out through the window without really seeing the pale, moonlit paddocks and the extravagant dusting of stars that formed the Milky Way.

He'd misjudged Camille Devereaux. She'd conned him. Kissed him and conned him with equal success. Hell! She was no better than Suzanne Heath.

He was fed up to the back teeth with this whole magazine business. From the moment he'd first discovered the bachelor nonsense, he'd taken a tough stand. He'd gone into defence mode—drawn a line in the sand—and not one of those scheming, husband-hunting women had been allowed to cross it.

Until Camille.

Damn it! He'd been on the brink of starting something with her. Scant minutes ago, all he'd been able to think of was wanting her, needing her, needing to get to know her, wanting to make love to her, wanting to find a way to keep her in his life.

He hadn't cared about the distance between Sydney and Mullinjim. In the twenty-first century a few thousand kilometres were not a major problem.

But duplicity was a problem.

Falling for a woman who strung you along with promises and lies was the very worst kind of problem. He had thought he'd already learned that lesson from Suzanne. Why hadn't he followed his initial hunch about Camille, that like all city journalists she was motivated by self-interest?

Somehow he'd fooled himself into thinking she was different. It was pathetic the way a man could let his hormones cloud clear thinking.

A hand on his arm startled him and he spun around

to find her standing close behind him, her face gleaming palely in the moon-touched darkness, her eyes deep, unfathomable pools.

'Had a nice little chat with Edith?' he asked scornfully.

'You mustn't take any notice of Edith,' she said.

'Why the hell not? She's your boss, isn't she?'

'Yes, but she's not writing this story. I am and I gave you my word, Jonno. I promised we'd drop you.'

'Did you tell *her* that?'

She sighed. 'I tried.'

'You tried,' he repeated in his most scathing, mocking tone. 'Good one, Camille. So next you'll be telling me, you're sorry, you did your best, but too bad.'

'No!' She crossed her arms over her chest and squared her shoulders, making her movements very deliberate as if to strengthen her argument. 'I'm doing exactly what I said I would. I'm writing an alternative outback story. Edith will buy it when she reads it and she'll get over her disappointment about you.'

'But that's not a given, is it? She's still expecting me to play along and you're still taking a gamble on this new story.'

'I promise that as soon as I get back I'll—'

'That's not the bargain you struck with me.'

She threw her head back and let out a sigh as she looked up to a point on the ceiling. 'It's *my* problem, Jonno. I won't let it impact on you. But, yes, I gambled. I have a motto: when you have no alternative, take a gamble!'

'There's always an alternative.'

'Oh yes,' she responded tartly. 'And the magazine's sales could drop through the floor. I could lose my job. Some alternatives aren't too appealing.'

He didn't answer. She'd just consolidated his worst fears.

There was no laughter from kookaburras the next morning. Just chubby fingers trying to pry Camille's eyes apart.

'Are you awake?' asked Bella.

'I am now.' Camille squinted sleepily and saw a fringe of blonde hair and two round green eyes peering at her over the edge of the bed.

'Can I get into your bed?'

'Oh, well...I guess so.'

Like an eager puppy, the little girl scrambled up and over Camille. 'You're lucky,' she said. 'You've had Megs sleeping on your bed.'

'Yes,' Camille said, smiling in spite of the early hour. 'She's been like a hot-water bottle on my feet all night. It was lovely.' She'd never had an animal sleep on her bed before. She'd never had a child *in* her bed either. Bella was already a warm little presence snuggled right in close under the bedclothes.

'I like your pyjamas,' the little girl said. 'I like red, shiny material.'

'But my pyjamas haven't got lovely black and white cows on them like yours. Yours are terrific.'

Bella beamed. 'I've got another pair at home with green frogs on them. I've got six dogs at home, too.'

'Lucky you.'

'How many dogs have you got?'

'None. Unless you count a little china French poodle that my dad gave me when I was little.'

'What's a French poodle?'

'It's the kind of dog people who live in France have.'

'Can they chase cattle?'

'Oh, no.' Camille laughed aloud at the thought. 'I think a French poodle would be frightened to death if it saw a cow. But I'll be able to take a photo of a poodle for you soon. I'm flying to France to visit my dad.'

'My daddy can fly up and down and sideways.'

'Your daddy's very clever with his helicopters, isn't he?' Camille couldn't believe she was actually enjoying this conversation.

'He's got four helichoppers.' Bella counted off four plump fingers and suddenly zoomed them into the air and landed them firmly on Camille's nose.

'Hey, my nose isn't a helipad,' Camille cried, but she was laughing and Bella was giggling as she swooped more helicopter fingers into Camille's curls.

'Bella!' called Jonno's voice from outside and their laughter died.

'We're in here, Uncle Jonno,' the little girl called.

'Where?'

There was a shadow in the bedroom doorway.

'Me and Camille is talking.'

Jonno peered around the doorway, frowning at them and Camille pulled the sheet tightly under her chin.

'Camille's my new best friend,' Bella announced.

He looked confused and upset and glared at them.

'Your breakfast's getting cold,' he said to Bella, and

he left again quickly without a word of greeting for
Camille.

And after he'd left Camille realised that she'd been
laughing this morning. She would have liked to explain
the significance of that to Jonno, but she knew he no
longer cared.

CHAPTER FIVE

CAMILLE was shocked to find how unsettled she felt when she returned to Sydney.

She sat at the window of her basement flat and stared at the streetscape outside and realised that she'd changed. Before she'd been to the outback it had never bothered her that the street-level view from her flat provided no glimpse of sky or trees.

Buildings, people, cars, pavement and the occasional pampered dog had been enough. She'd always been happy to start the day sitting here in her tiny breakfast nook, drinking coffee and watching the world go by.

The world. As if the world comprised the swish and screech of vehicles' tyres, the frantic tattoo of women's heels on the pavement, the slouching shuffle of teenagers' dirty sneakers, or the arrogant strides of corporate commandos wearing the latest in hand-stitched leather.

What was wrong with her? Why, after four months, was she still hankering for something else? For the pungent scent of wattle or even the dusky smell of cattle pens, the raucous laughter of kookaburras, or a glimpse of the rich, rosy underside of galahs' wings as they chased each other across wide, wide blue skies?

The sight of a tall, dark cattleman with a dangerous, reluctant smile?

It was such a waste of head-space to continue storing

memories of Edenvale. After all, her brief interlude in the bush was well and truly behind her.

There had been no fond farewells when she left. Jonno had been as terse and grim as when they'd met and so she'd accepted Piper's invitation to visit Windaroo and had done the rest of her research there.

And she hadn't heard from Jonno since she left.

Not once.

She'd sent him a polite letter soon after she returned to Sydney, thanking him for his hospitality, and a postcard a couple of months later, on the pretext that she was curious to know how her steers were faring.

The only reply had been a brief, perfunctory letter from Jonno's agent, Andrew Bowen, informing her that if current weather patterns and market conditions held, Jonathan Rivers had advised him to sell her stock in approximately six weeks time.

Six weeks. The edition of *Girl Talk* with her story about Mullinjim would have hit the stands by then. Camille's mouth turned dry as she remembered the battle she'd had with Edith.

'Think juxtaposition, Edith,' she'd pleaded. 'If we put this outback story and the bachelor story side-by-side, the readers won't mind that Jonno's gone because we'll have given them something else to think about.'

She'd been sure it would work if they accompanied her story with plenty of glossy pictures of fit-looking, attractive outback men—bachelors, married men, family men.

Edith, thank God, had finally agreed, with a warning

that if it didn't work Camille's head would be served to their publishers on a platter.

In the long run it had been Camille's closest friend, Jen, a fellow *Girl Talk* journalist, who had been her biggest problem. She'd pestered her for the real goss about Jonno.

What was he like in the flesh? What about his personality? What was Camille covering up about him? Had she made a move on him? She had, hadn't she? She was keeping him for herself...

Eventually...*eventually*, Jen had given up.

Now Camille had six weeks to wait till the story was published...and six weeks till her brief career in the cattle industry and all connection with Jonno Rivers came to an end.

In six weeks' time she could get back to normal.

Jonno might have guessed that his sister-in-law would bring up the topic of Camille the minute he set foot in her kitchen.

'So what did you think of Camille's article in *Girl Talk*?' she asked.

'Is that why you invited me to dinner? To grill me?'

'No!' Piper managed to look offended. 'I invited you because we haven't seen you for ages. I bet you didn't even know that Michael's started crawling. He'll be walking soon.'

'Really?' Jonno felt genuinely shocked. 'Sorry. I've been rather busy.'

Piper frowned up at him and her eyes held his in a

bold blue stare. 'That's the flimsy excuse I gave Camille.'

'*You what?*' He struggled to breathe. 'You've been talking to her?'

She turned back to the stove and stirred a pot of bacon and mushroom soup. 'I rang her to thank her for sending us a complimentary copy of *Girl Talk* and to congratulate her on a great story.'

'I—I see.'

'She was delighted to hear from me and of course she asked what *you* thought of the story.'

Jonno tried to swallow the brick in his throat. 'That soup smells sensational.'

'Jonno!' Piper cried impatiently. 'Just remember, I know you Rivers men. Changing the subject won't wash with me.'

He sighed. 'OK, OK. So Camille wanted to know what I thought of her article. What did you tell her?'

Piper winced. 'I'm afraid I didn't handle it as smoothly as I would have liked. She caught me out. I kind of stammered and spluttered for a bit, then I think I mumbled something about how busy you'd been and that we hadn't seen you.'

Jonno nodded.

'And naturally she guessed I was covering for you.'

'You weren't covering anything. You were telling her the truth.'

She sent him an old-fashioned look. 'Whatever you say, Jonno, but I reckon you owe me an answer now. What *did* you think of Camille's article?'

He scowled at her. 'I don't make a habit of reading chicks' magazines.'

'Oh, give me a break. This isn't just any magazine. This is the story Camille was planning when she was here! When she was living under your roof!'

Jonno half expected Piper to add 'when you were giving her mouth-to-mouth resuscitation for a scratch on the chin', but to his relief she merely said, 'She sent you a copy, didn't she?'

He sighed. 'Yes, but it's still in its plastic wrapper. I'm not interested in it, Piper. I'm sick of the whole bloody affair.'

She gazed at him without speaking for long, nerve-racking seconds. 'I'm sorry to hear that.' Her expression was thoughtful as she turned back to the stove. 'I really liked Camille,' she said over her shoulder.

He knew she was expecting a response, but he refused to oblige her and he couldn't provide a logical explanation for his behaviour either. It was more a gut-level knowledge that thinking about Camille, reading her story, would start his inner turmoil again. And he'd had enough of that.

But he hadn't bargained on his sister-in-law's persistence. Setting the wooden spoon aside, she turned to face him, her face serious, her eyes shimmering with tender concern. 'Camille is nothing like Suzanne Heath, Jonno. I'm quite certain of that.'

He couldn't comment. Piper meant well, but he knew better and besides, even if she was right, he couldn't take a risk on Camille. He'd known from the minute he met her that she was dangerous. He'd heard alarms ringing right from the start, warning him that she would be addictive.

She *was* addictive. After he kissed her, he went mad with wanting more. It was much safer to settle for nothing.

He wasn't sure how long he stood there, like a mute fool in the middle of Piper's kitchen, but he heard her loud sigh. Next minute she grabbed a pile of soup bowls and spoons from the counter and shoved them into his hands. 'Make yourself useful. Put these on the table.' And as he headed for the dining room, she called after him, 'While you're in there, select a nice red to go with this meal.'

He was removing the cork from a fine South Australian bottle when Gabe came into the room bearing a platter of home-baked bread, followed by Piper with the steaming soup.

'What's eating you two?' Gabe asked, his eyes glinting with curious amusement as he looked from his wife's determined expression to his brother's mulish obstinacy.

'I've been telling Jonno that he's mad not to read Camille's article,' Piper said.

Gabe's eyebrows shot high with surprise. 'You haven't read it, Jonno? You should. She did a terrific job!'

'So I've heard,' Jonno said gruffly.

As they took their places Gabe said, 'No, honestly, mate, I was impressed.'

'I don't know how Camille managed to include so much realism and still capture the romance of living in the bush, but she did it. It's brilliant,' chimed in Piper.

'And she handled your withdrawal from that bachelor caper very tactfully as well,' Gabe added as he filled Jonno's wine glass.

'She *what*?' Jonno's head jerked up as he stared at his brother. 'So she kept her word?'

'Of course she flaming well did,' said Gabe. 'I reckon that was the point of the article.' He sent Jonno a teasing grin. 'She needed something in the magazine to help those poor readers get over their bitter, heart-rending disappointment at losing out on you.'

'Well, it's about time they learned the score,' Jonno growled, hoping to hide his sudden confusion. 'At least now the whole sorry business can be finished with.'

'Camille, it's Cynthia in Reception. There's a man down here asking for you.'

Camille groaned into the phone. She was in deadline hell, racing to get a story finished, and her afternoon had been interrupted by far too many calls.

'Do you know what he wants?' she asked, holding the receiver awkwardly between her shoulder and her ear while keeping her eyes glued to her computer screen and her hands poised above the keyboard.

'No.'

Camille smiled with relief. Good old Cynthia. Her lack of initiative meant she was a ho-hum receptionist, but on days like this it was a blessing. 'Sorry, Cynth. I'm up to my eyeballs. This story was due in this morning. The subs are screaming for my blood. I can't see anyone. He'll have to leave a message or see someone else.'

'OK,' Cynthia replied in her singsong voice.

'Thanks, mate.' Camille dropped the receiver and continued typing furiously. She'd just had a terrific idea for the final paragraph—a succinct and witty summing-up. It was brilliant!

One sentence was down when a clattering of heels on the stairs intruded her peace and Jen dashed into the office.

'Camille,' she shouted, 'I can't believe you sent your cowboy bachelor away.'

'What?' Camille stared at Jen blankly, her mind still deep in her story. 'What did you say?'

'Your outback lover-boy was downstairs just now asking for you and you told Cynthia to send him away!'

'Jonno?' *My God! Oh, my God!* A flood of adrenaline swamped her as if she'd just had one of those naked-in-the-office nightmares. 'You mean that caller Cynthia phoned about was Jonathan Rivers? Are you sure? Why didn't Cynth say so?'

She couldn't think. *Jonno.* Her heart began to pound.

'Oh, you know what a goose Cynthia is! She didn't have the wits to keep him talking. I'd just come in from a job as this gorgeous hunk walked out. By the time it dawned on me who he was, it was too late. I scorched back into the street, ready to chase after him, but he'd already disappeared.'

'Goodness, Jen,' Camille said as her breathing began to settle and common sense returned. 'I'm glad you didn't chase him. What on earth would you have said?'

Jen smirked. 'Darling, that's for me to know and for you to find out.'

Camille turned back to her screen. *Get a grip, girl! This is nothing to get excited about.* He was probably in the city on business and had dropped by to tell her that the sale of the steers had gone through.

She flashed Jen a tight smile. 'I couldn't have seen him anyway. I'm way past my deadline. I shouldn't even be taking time out to talk to you now.'

Jenny shook her head. 'My dear Millie, no deadline is that important. Jonno Rivers is a god. You mustn't turn your back on divine intervention.'

'That's pitiful, Jen,' Camille said, staring vaguely at her screen. Blast! She still hadn't typed her brilliant final paragraph and for the life of her she couldn't remember one word of it.

Cynthia was closing down Reception by the time Camille had e-mailed the finished story through to a sub-editor.

She hurled herself downstairs just as the receptionist was heading out the front door.

'Hey, Cynth, wait!'

The girl hesitated in the doorway, looking back over her shoulder.

'Sorry to hold you up,' Camille panted. 'About that guy who was asking for me—'

Cynthia smiled. 'The really cute one?'

'I understand it was Jonathan Rivers. Did he…?' She tried not to sound too anxious. 'Did he leave a message…at all?'

'Oh, yeah. He left an envelope.' Cynthia pointed across the foyer. 'I put it in your pigeon-hole.'

Camille's eyes swivelled to the bank of pigeon-holes on the far wall. 'Oh, great. Thanks a million.'

'That's OK,' Cynthia replied, intrigued, then with a shrug she continued out of the building as Camille was already diving for the pigeon-holes.

Her heart stuttered when she saw her name written in bold black handwriting on the front of an envelope. She tried to remember if she'd seen Jonno's writing. It seemed familiar. The envelope felt rather empty, and at first she thought there was nothing inside, but when she slit it open a cardboard ticket fell out.

A ticket to the opera house.

How weird. Her brow wrinkled as she stared at the little cardboard rectangle. A performance of the Sydney Symphony Orchestra! Jonno and symphony orchestras? Somehow the two didn't match. Perhaps Cynthia had made a mistake. Someone else had left this and there was another message from Jonno.

She checked everyone else's pigeon-holes.

No other mail for her.

She ran her fingers around the inside of the envelope, hoping for a note—some kind of explanation—but there was nothing except the ticket.

What on earth should she do? The concert was tonight at the main concert hall of the opera house. If only she'd spoken to Jonno. Heavens, she wasn't even certain that the man who'd left this ticket was *him*. She hadn't heard from him in all this time.

But Jen had been convinced.

Sinking into a chair, she stared at the ticket. The performance started at eight o'clock. She would be pushing it to get home, changed, and back to Circular Quay in time for a dignified arrival at the opera house.

And did she want to go? She didn't dislike symphony orchestras, but heavens, she didn't even know if Jonno would be there. Then again, surely he wouldn't leave her a ticket to go on her own?

Her mind buzzed like a frenzied mosquito as she grabbed her things and headed onto the street. Why was she so excited? The ticket could have been dropped off by anyone. People hoping for publicity were always sending tickets to the *Girl Talk* office.

Cynthia didn't have a clue. Jen had never actually seen Jonno in the flesh so she might have been mistaken. Camille shook her head. This was crazy! Here she was with her pulse racing, breaking out in a cold sweat—over nothing.

And if Jonno was in town handing out concert tickets—how rude! How dared he suddenly turn up here without warning. She'd put her heart and soul into writing that article to get him off the hook and there hadn't been a word of thanks!

While her train sped her homewards, she calmed down and decided she wouldn't go. It had taken a supreme effort over several months before she'd finally mastered the art of putting Jonno Rivers right out of her mind.

But she'd done it. She was over him.

Heavens, if she really analysed their history there'd been nothing to get over. One kiss! They'd had one interrupted kiss. And if she went out tonight, she would get all stirred up again.

Over nothing. Nothing.

She was just going down the steps to her front door

when she heard her phone ringing. Frantically she jumped the last two steps, then completely fumbled getting her key in the lock and took ten times longer than usual to get inside. And of course the ringing stopped just as she reached the phone.

Camille groaned, but then she heard a rich, gravelly voice speaking on her answering machine.

'Camille. Jonno Rivers here. I hope you got the ticket to the show. Sorry this is short notice, and I'm afraid I'm going to be tied up with meetings until almost eight, so I can't leave you a number to call and I won't be able to pick you up. Could we meet in the foyer? Hope I see you there.'

Camille played the message through again.

Just hearing his voice made her feel suddenly hollow inside and close to tears. Jonno really was here in Sydney.

What should she do?

This was the kind of dating dilemma she was supposed to advise others about. Last year she'd written a series for *Girl Talk* called 'The A to Z of Dating Strategies'.

N is for No, the most important word in your dating vocabulary. *N* is also for Never. Never accept last-minute invitations. You don't want to give out the message that you have nothing better to do. You're *never* that desperate.

Of course she shouldn't go.

She wouldn't.

Jonno wasn't even interested enough to read her outback article.

She would stay home tonight and get a Thai take-away and rent a soppy, chick-flick video. No, nothing romantic. It would only make her more messed up. She'd get an action adventure or a psychological thriller.

Feeling slightly calmer, she drifted through her flat towards her bedroom. She felt completely wrung out...as if she'd battled her way through a storm at sea.

And she felt disembodied somehow... It was as if the part of her who had just decided to stay at home was a spectator watching another Camille from the side-lines...watching that other self fling open her wardrobe doors and gaze at her line-up of clothes...

And as she watched she saw that other Camille's hands lift out her little black silk number and her red velvet...

And she watched with a puzzled frown as she put the black dress back in the closet and laid the red velvet on her bed.

CHAPTER SIX

WHICH foyer? Camille wasn't a regular patron of the concert hall of the Sydney Opera House, and it was only after she'd arrived this evening that she'd discovered there was a foyer for each compass point.

She supposed Jonno couldn't have known that the opera house was so huge or he would have suggested a more specific meeting place. Within the Northern Foyer alone there was the Granite Level, the Mural Level, the Bar Level and this splendid-looking purple Lounge Level.

Hovering at the top of an imposing purple-carpeted staircase, she scanned the sea of theatre-goers who'd gathered below to laugh and chat, or wave their programmes to each other.

She'd expected Jonno to be easy to find. Surely his distinctive stature would stand out from the crowd? But she couldn't find him among the scores of tall men, all dressed alike in black evening suits, and a sudden thought brought her hands to her mouth. Maybe she was looking at the wrong guys.

Jonno mightn't own formal evening clothes. Perhaps she should be looking for jeans and riding boots. Crumbs. He wouldn't wear his akubra to the opera house, would he?

She glanced at her watch. Ten to eight.

With two thousand people to seat in the massive hall, the ushers would be getting toey. She should be moving inside.

Could Jonno be lost?

Chances were he knew next to nothing about finding his way around in the city. She still managed to get lost at times.

Then again—perhaps this was all a joke.

Had she been stood up?

Would Jonno do a thing like that? Was he still terribly angry with her?

In the midst of her panic it occurred to Camille that perhaps he had given up waiting out here and had taken his seat. That had to be what had happened! Once more she checked her ticket and hurried through the appropriate door. But their seats were empty and when she darted back outside the woman at the door glared at her.

'You'll need to be seated soon or you won't be allowed back into the auditorium,' she said icily. 'Then you'll have to watch the closed-circuit televisions in the Southern Foyer until there's an interval.'

'Oh, dear,' Camille said. 'I'm not sure what to do. I'm waiting for someone.'

She was on the edge of tears. The whole evening had been so bizarre. First there'd been the shock of Jonno turning up at the office, then the mysterious envelope and missing him on the telephone…her hasty decision to come and the mad scramble to get here on time…

Now this.

She wandered back to one of the main doors opening onto the forecourt outside. From there she could see people hurrying through the night as they came along the walkway from Circular Quay and to her right she could see Sydney Harbour with its splendid necklace of glittering lights. Beyond the Rocks, the harbour bridge's familiar coat-hanger silhouette spanned the silky black water.

It might have been nice to share these views with Jonno.

Rubbish! She'd been crazy to come. She should have stayed with her first instincts and had a cosy night at home with Pad Thai noodles and a video.

Stuff Jonno!

Sighing loudly, she turned back to the brightly lit foyer and saw a tall, dark tuxedo-clad figure dashing towards the auditorium doors just as they were closing.

Her heart jumped. 'Jonno!' She hurried forward.

He didn't hear her.

'Jonno!' She waved to catch his attention as she ran.

But he didn't look her way. She caught a glimpse of the charming, one-sided smile he offered the usher and saw the woman beaming back at him as she took him inside the already darkened theatre.

When she was a mere six feet from the door it closed with a sharp click.

'Come back! Let me in!' Tears of frustration stung her eyes as she jiggled the door handle, but no one came.

Jonno made his way through the darkened auditorium, past people's knees with the usual mutterings of 'Excuse me'. Halfway along the row, he saw the two empty red plush seats.

Camille hadn't come.

He whirled around and saw the doors behind him were firmly closed.

'Can you please take your seat?' someone hissed.

He considered storming back out of the theatre. Would it be bad form to demand an exit just as the orchestra's conductor appeared on the stage?

He gritted his teeth. He was caught in a trap of his own making. That damn meeting with the Cattle Council had gone on far too long and hadn't left him any time to search the foyer, but he'd assumed that Camille would have taken her seat by now.

Of course, he'd been taking a crazy gamble that she would come at all. She would have a thousand very good reasons why she shouldn't—a thousand and one better things to do tonight than dash out on an impromptu date with a bloke from the bush she hadn't seen for months. Most likely she was out with a boyfriend, some guy selected from her long string of available partners.

He shouldn't have listened to Piper and Gabe. Shouldn't have read Camille's article about marriage in the outback. Shouldn't have read and reread her story until he was certain that she was reaching out to him, speaking to him from the page.

He'd been carried away, thinking that as he read he could hear her voice. See her smile. Feel her lips on his. Sense her longing.

The opening strains of a symphony flowed over and around him. Stirring emotional stuff. Just what he didn't need right now. A deep sigh escaped and the man next to him frowned.

Only an hour to wait till intermission.

*   *   *

'What can I get you?' The dapper barman pushed a drinks menu towards Camille.

Perched on a tall stool, she scanned it and sent him a regretful smile. 'Well, there's one cocktail on that list that's definitely meant for me.'

'And what's that?'

'A Dirty Cowboy.'

'Ah.' He smiled knowingly. 'From the way you said that, it sounds like you know one or two cowboys.'

'Just one,' she said. 'And believe me, one's enough.'

As he mixed butterscotch schnapps and Baileys, he asked, 'Did you get here too late for the concert?'

'No,' she sighed. 'The cowboy did. But now he's inside and I'm stuck out here.'

'I suppose that makes sense,' he said, frowning doubtfully.

Camille shook her head. 'No, it doesn't. It doesn't make any sense at all, but don't worry, nothing's making sense tonight.'

He placed her drink carefully in front of her. 'Did you know you could watch the show from the Southern Foyer?'

'Yes,' Camille said. She took a sip and smiled. 'Oh, this is decadent.'

The barman smiled back. 'Relax and enjoy it, love. And don't worry, I've heard that the second half of this concert will be the best.'

At interval, when Jonno saw the woman sitting on her own in a corner of the bar, he couldn't help taking a second glance. The deep V of her low-backed, dark red velvet dress revealed pale skin that looked as fine as alabaster against the richness of the fabric.

It took several seconds to register that he knew the owner of that admirable back.

'Camille!'

She swung around so quickly that the drink in her hand splashed onto the bar top. Her hair had grown. Glossy, soft curls reached almost to her shoulders. Her eyes were made up to look dramatic. She looked sophisticated beyond belief. He felt rooted to the spot by her beauty.

'Jonno,' she said, her cheeks flushing swiftly. 'Fancy seeing you here.'

'You've come.' He was taken aback by how incredibly happy he felt to be seeing her again after all these months.

'Is it interval already?' she asked, casting a nervous glance at the crowds filing into the bar.

'Yes.' He stepped closer to her. 'Have you been here long?'

'Ages.' She raised her glass and sent him a wistful smile and he wondered how much she'd had to drink.

'I'm really sorry I missed you before the concert started. I was held up at a cattlemen's meeting.' He touched her arm. 'I wasn't sure you would come.'

'Neither was I.' She shook her head and looked at his hand on her arm and then smiled at him from beneath dusky lashes. 'I'm still not sure *why* I came.'

Her gaze lifted slightly so that her dark eyes looked

with uncompromising directness straight into his and he could sense the questions she wanted to ask about why he'd turned up in Sydney out of the blue and why he'd invited her to this concert, but he hoped she would leave those questions unasked. He might frighten her off if he told her.

'What are you drinking?' he asked.

Her expression took on a taunting cheekiness. 'I'm having Dirty Cowboys in honour of you, Jonno.'

A barman appeared behind her and he appraised Jonno with a surprised head-to-toe glance and released a low whistle. 'This isn't your cowboy, is it, love?'

She blushed. 'He's not exactly *my* cowboy.'

'Perhaps we should go back inside,' Jonno said, taking the glass from her hand and setting it on the bar.

She sighed. 'Yes, too many drinks make me sleepy, and I suppose you want to hear the second half of the concert.'

'It's the best part.'

'So I've heard.' As she slid from the stool, she frowned up at him. 'I didn't know you liked classical music.'

'A friend of mine is playing tonight. He sent me the tickets.'

'Oh.' Her eyebrows arched in surprise. 'So that's why you came to Sydney.'

'Partly. I had business as well...'

She seemed a little put out by his reply and began to walk ahead of him.

'Camille,' he said.

She turned back.

'I haven't told you how beautiful you look tonight. You look amazing!'

He saw a fresh bloom of pink sweep up from her neck to her cheeks. 'Thanks.' She smiled shyly and sent an admiring glance that took in his formal evening clothes. 'So do you.'

And that's an understatement, Camille thought.

In the outback, Jonno's shoulders had looked splendid in a cotton shirt, but tonight they looked downright incredible in a tuxedo. As for his suntan, his posture, his cheekbones, she just wanted to stare and stare.

And his smile. Oh, help, his smile undid her. How could she pretend that she didn't know why she'd come? She felt electrified just to walk with him into the theatre, to sit beside him.

But why had he invited her? Was this a date or did he simply need to be seen at the theatre with an escort?

'Which one is your friend?' she whispered as the members of the orchestra came onto the stage, took their seats and began to tune their instruments.

'He's not there yet,' Jonno said, leaning towards her so that she caught a delicious whiff of his aftershave. 'He's the soloist.'

'Oh,' she said, her eyes widening. 'Jonno, I'm impressed.'

She hadn't looked at a programme, so she had no idea who this evening's soloist was. A violinist, perhaps? Or a tenor? She was about to ask what his friend played when an expectant buzz rippled through the audience and the house lights dimmed.

Applause broke out as the grey-haired conductor

walked onto the stage and then there was even louder applause for the man who followed him—a tall, proud young Aborigine carrying a didgeridoo.

Camille shot a surprised sideways glance to Jonno and he turned, smiled and winked.

Whatever she'd expected when she set off for the opera house this evening, she hadn't thought she'd be blown away by a unique musical experience, but from the moment the didgeridoo player appeared on stage she was entranced.

The humble native instrument, made from a tree branch hollowed out by white ants and decorated with tribal patterns in red, black, yellow and white paint, provided a striking contrast to the elegant, highly varnished European violins and cellos and the gleaming golden brass trumpets and horns.

And once the music started she was transfixed by its thrilling, soul-stirring sound... She'd heard Aboriginal music before, but never in this combination.

Tonight the pungent earthiness of the didgeridoo droned against the sweetness of violins. It was like a throbbing, dark, pulsing voice from an ancient, forty-thousand-year-old culture breaking through into a new world.

Camille felt the music reach into her and touch her in a way that turned her skin to goose-bumps and lifted fine hairs on the back of her neck. Tears clogged her throat. It was as if the haunting, remote outback was right here in the midst of slick, modern and self-important Sydney.

She felt incredibly aware of Jonno's strong, silent

presence beside her. Like the music, he came from another world. And she remembered with a pang the
strange, unexpected sense of belonging she'd felt when
she'd been at Edenvale.

She suspected she was in love with him, but hoped to
heavens she wasn't.

As they left the concert hall her emotions were tum-
bling and bubbling so fiercely she felt ready to burst.
'That was sheer magic,' she said breathlessly.

'It was, wasn't it? I'm glad you could come.'

'How long have you known the didgeridoo player?'

'William Tudmara? Since we were kids. Three generations of his family have worked as stockmen on
Edenvale, and when we realised how talented Billy was
my family went in to bat for him. We organised sponsors
and contacts, and Billy's taken to the limelight like a
duck to a swamp.'

'Wow!' Camille drew in a sharp breath. What would
Jonno think if he'd known that she'd been worrying he
might not know what to *wear* to the opera house?
Heavens, he was a patron of the soloist! 'Are you going
backstage to congratulate your friend?'

His gaze travelled over her hungrily, making her
shiver. 'I caught up with Billy after his rehearsal this
morning. Tonight he'll have so many bigwigs fussing
around him he won't miss us. I'll ring him tomorrow.'

'Please thank him for my ticket. I loved his music. It
was incredibly moving.' Incredibly sexy, she thought,
but felt too self-conscious to say so.

'I'll tell him.' He took her hand in his and turned from
the brightly lit foyer to look out into the night, then he

dipped his mouth to her ear. 'How about we slip away?' His hand squeezed hers. 'Just the two of us.'

Camille swallowed.

She tried to remember all the reasons she had to be cautious about Jonno. Their bitter parting. The months of silence...

And she reminded herself that he was dangerous. She barely knew him and yet he had a hold on her that was scary. He'd kissed her once and cast a spell over her so that she'd been unable to forget him.

And now it was happening again. Perhaps it was the tension of waiting...or the cocktails...or the amazing music... She couldn't tell. But all it took was a squeeze of his hand and there was only one answer that made any sense. 'Come back to my place.'

His eyes searched her face and she flashed hot and cold. They both knew they were talking about more than another kiss.

'Sure,' he said without smiling.

They hardly spoke as their taxi sped through the inky, neon-splashed streets. They were too tense, too burning, too anxious. Camille kept stealing little glances Jonno's way, and each time she saw him she felt completely overwhelmed. This was Jonno Rivers, the most desirable of all *Girl Talk*'s heartthrob bachelors.

And here he was in Sydney. In a taxi with *her. Coming back to her flat.*

The cab drew up in front of her apartment block and Jonno paid the driver while her heart sped and skipped as she hunted in her bag for her key.

When they entered her flat, she didn't even bother to

offer him coffee. She dumped her bag and keys on the kitchen counter and turned to find that Jonno was already reaching for her.

And she fell into his open arms with a glad, helpless cry.

He gathered her close and excitement darted through her in a shower of sparks as she felt the steel strength of his muscles beneath his coat and smelled his crisp, clean shirt and the warm, woodsy musk of his after-shave.

'You've no idea how many times I've thought about this,' he whispered.

'Ditto,' she whispered back.

Hadn't she been dreaming for months about how it would feel if he kissed her again?

And here he was, leaning back against her kitchen cupboards and drawing her close so that her hips were hard against him as he lowered his mouth to hers and his hard arousal pressed into her while his lips and tongue did warm, soft and mesmerising things to her mouth.

How could she think about the wisdom of this? She couldn't worry about the future or what this could mean when she was turning to sweet, wild liquid in his arms!

'I want you,' he growled against her lips in a voice that sent heat flooding through her veins, swirling and licking into every secret part of her.

I want you, too. She couldn't quite bring herself to say the words out loud, so she boldly took his hand and led the way to her bedroom, stopping every few steps of the journey down the hall for taste tests and nibbles and eager scatterings of hungry kisses.

By the light of her ruby glass bedside lamp, they undressed each other with fumbling, impatient hands. Every so often they looked into each other's eyes and exchanged, shy, excited smiles, and kissed some more.

Camille's red dress slipped to the carpet with a soft, velvety sigh and Jonno's sure fingers explored the lines of her bare shoulders. Where his fingers trailed, his lips followed, tracing a path of hot delight from her shoulder to her collar-bone, then oh, oh, bliss—her breasts.

They sank together onto the bed, breathless and shaking with wanting each other. She had never felt so swept away with desire. It was frightening to feel so out of control and yet it didn't matter. This was Jonno and he felt so, so good.

Nothing that felt this right could be a mistake.

Jonno woke first. He'd been sleeping with an arm draped possessively over Camille's breasts and now he lay very still as he watched daylight spill through a high dormer window into her messy bedroom. Pieces of clothing were scattered from one end of the room to the other, bringing back memories of the miracle of their night together.

He'd been overwhelmed by the intensity of his emotions as he made love to Camille. He'd experienced passion before, sure, but it had never been tempered by such an exquisite tenderness, so sweet it was almost painful.

Beside him Camille stirred and her eyes opened slowly. 'Hi, there,' she said, and her lips curved in a sleepy, secretive smile as she looked around and remembered, too.

'Good morning.' He kissed the tip of her nose and allowed his thumb to glide lazily over her nipple, felt it tighten beneath his touch.

Camille stretched deliciously and sighed. 'I wish I didn't have to go to work today. No one should ever have to go to work after a night like last night.'

'Don't go,' he murmured, sliding his hand down over the smooth curve of her hip.

'I have to. I'm already behind schedule this week.'

'Did you know you look tumbled and rumpled and sexy as hell?'

'Do I?' She laughed and gave a little shake of her head so that her curls fell every which way over her face.

'Oh, God, Camille,' he groaned, lifting her hair away from her eyes and kissing her. 'I could become fatally addicted to waking up next to you.'

She sat up quickly, her face suddenly wary. 'Well, I can't see that happening, can you? I'll get breakfast. Will coffee and toast do?'

'Sure.'

One look at the tight, suddenly anxious expression on her face and he rejected his impulse to pull her down beside him and make love to her yet again.

Instead, he contented himself with watching her as she slipped quickly out of bed and pulled an oversized T-shirt over her head and he admired the way the thin fabric clung to her breasts and her bottom as she walked out of the room. But when she was gone, he was left with a rush of doubts and a gut-wrenching uneasiness.

* * *

They met for lunch at an exclusive harbourside restaurant with walls of glass offering views of the spectacular, tiered sails of the opera house on Bennelong Point. Below them ferries and sailing boats criss-crossed the sparkling, bright blue water.

After they were seated, Camille said, 'My workmate, Jen, has guessed that I'm seeing you and she's carrying on about how I got you out of the bachelor project so I could keep you for myself.'

Jonno grinned. 'You did, didn't you?'

She blushed and looked away. 'You know that wasn't my plan at the time.'

She was grateful he didn't ask her what she planned now, because she couldn't have answered. She didn't have a plan. All she knew was that Jonno had bounced back into her life and she was falling for him. Fast. Deeply. Totally.

She glanced towards the harbour bridge, where the moving traffic looked like coloured beads threaded along a string, and she frowned.

All morning she'd been growing more and more worried. She was afraid she was leading Jonno on. He was assuming that they might have a future.

But what kind of future could they have? Last night it had seemed so right, so poetic—as if they could blend their differences the way the music had.

But, in the hard light of day, she was no longer sure. She'd seen where Jonno came from—the land and the people who made up the environment that had nurtured him. She'd seen his family. Gabe and Piper. His love for his niece and nephew.

He might look like a pirate, but at heart he was the salt-of-the-earth type, the marrying kind. Piper had told her that he'd hoped his last girlfriend was carrying his child.

Despite his rejection of 'The Bachelor Project', he really wanted all that…marriage and a family.

Whereas she…

The waiter came to take their orders and as he left Jonno said, 'I've been wondering about your family. Do they live in Sydney?'

She hesitated, caught out by how closely his thoughts mirrored hers.

'Sorry if that's an intrusive question,' he said, 'but you know all about me and my family. You've seen where I was born and where I've lived all my life.'

'You're not being intrusive, Jonno. It's the kind of normal, reasonable question people ask each other. It's just that…' She sighed. 'It's just that I don't have a normal family.'

'Oh, I see.' The skin around his eyes creased as he smiled. 'So you can't even hint at which solar system they live in?'

Camille laughed. 'OK. You win. My parents and I, and there's only the three of us, are about as scattered as possible. I'm the only one in Sydney. My mother's in Tokyo and my father's in Paris, I think.'

'You think?' He looked shocked.

'Well, Dad's based in Paris,' she said. 'But last time I heard from him he was château-sitting somewhere in the Loire valley.'

'I guess *château*-sitting would beat babysitting hands down.'

She grinned. 'Sounds pretentious, doesn't it? He was minding someone's house—a friend of his. A choreographer, or maybe it was a composer. I forget. Anyhow, that was over six months ago. I imagine he'd be back in Paris by now.'

The waiter came with champagne and glasses and made a little ceremony of popping the cork and pouring their wine.

'Cheers,' Jonno said, clinking his glass to Camille's.

Their gazes meshed and she thought of last night, of how exquisitely Jonno had made love to her, and just to think of it made her feel as if the champagne bubbles were already fizzing through her veins. 'What shall we drink to?' she asked quickly.

For a second or two she regretted asking that. Jonno's eyes seemed to look right inside her, as if she held the answer to her own question, but then he gave a little shake and lifted his glass and smiled. 'Let's drink to rising beef prices, so you can make a little profit on your steers.'

'So *we* can make a big profit on *our* steers,' Camille corrected. 'We're splitting fifty-fifty, remember?'

'OK. Here's to *our* steers,' he said. After they'd sipped their wine, he added, 'I'm afraid beef prices haven't been great lately. That's why I've been holding off from selling. You're not going to be excited about what we can make on fifteen steers.'

'As long as I still have enough to go to Paris.'

'To visit your father?'

'Yes. I've had my holidays booked for ages. I'm hoping to go next month.'

'Then we'd better get them to the market place,' he said gravely.

Camille took another sip of champagne. Why should telling Jonno that she was going away, even for a short time, make her feel uncomfortable?

'And did you say your mother lives in Japan?' he asked.

'That's right. She's artistic director of a contemporary-dance company in Tokyo.'

'So that explains it.'

'Explains what?'

'Why you seem…touched by something less ordinary. Your parents are both artistic.'

She shrugged and sent him a coy smile. 'There's nothing ordinary about you, Jonno.'

'Don't you believe it,' he said with a chuckle. 'But tell me about your parents.'

'Well, their names are Laine Sullivan and Fabrice Devereaux and they used to be ballet dancers. At one stage they were quite famous, but I don't suppose you've heard of them?'

'I'm afraid not.'

'Mum is Australian and Dad's French, but they danced as partners in companies all over the world.' She twisted the stem of her champagne flute. 'They could dance a *pas de deux* sublimely. But—but they couldn't live together in any kind of harmony. Their rows were terrible.'

'And so they've lived apart for some time?'

'They finally separated when I was fifteen, but they've never officially divorced.'

'It can't have been very pleasant for you.'

'No.' She let out an unusually deep sigh. 'So my family is very different from yours, isn't it?'

He lifted his glass in a salute. '*Vive la différence.* Part of the problem with living in the bush is that just about everyone has had much the same experience. We're born and bred in the district, we go away for a few years to boarding-school and perhaps university. Sometimes we do the overseas-travel thing, then we come back to work the land. End of story. All very boring really.'

He grinned. 'Gabe was a bit different. He went off to fly Black Hawks for several years, but there's not a château-sitter or artistic director among us.'

Camille smiled. 'There's a good side to "boring". It's very secure. I've often wondered if my parents' problem was that they were always jetting about on tour. There was never any sense of permanence in their lives.'

Their meals arrived and they paid attention to the delicious smoked fish cakes they'd both ordered and talked about the music of the night before and Jonno's friendship with Billy, the didgeridoo player.

'He's heading for a gig in New York next,' Jonno said, then he looked thoughtfully at Camille. 'Did you trail around with your parents when they toured?'

'I did when I was little, before I started boarding-school. I travelled all over the world, but all I remember is going from one hotel to another.'

He put down his knife and fork and shook his head as he looked at her. 'I'm trying to picture you as a little girl. Little Camille with big dark eyes and dark curly hair sitting on all those aeroplanes, hanging around in all those hotel lobbies...'

She gave him a tight-lipped smile. 'I was quite precocious. I learned to order Room Service before I was five.'

'But were you lonely?'

Oh, God, yes, she thought, but said, 'I made friends with hotel staff, and some of the backstage crew were very good to me. The lighting guy was my favourite. He used to let me sit with him at rehearsals sometimes and there was one switch I was allowed to work.'

She sat back, hands in her lap, and stared at him, surprised that she'd told him so much. She hardly ever spilled her heart out about all this. Next minute she'd be giving him a full inventory of her insecurities, and then where would they be?

'Did you ever want a different life?' he asked.

'You bet. I was very jealous of ordinary kids.' She took a sip of wine and looked out across the dazzling harbour again. 'Do you know what I used to long for?'

'Tell me.'

'To have a house with a garden, so I could have a hose fight.'

He laughed.

'I can remember being in a taxi with my parents, driving through the suburbs of New Orleans on the way to yet another hotel, and I saw children playing in their front yard. They were in their swimsuits and they were squirting each other with water and I thought it was the most exciting, fun thing I'd ever seen.'

Jonno leaned forward and took her hands in his. 'A hose fight is a fantasy I could help you with,' he said in a voice that was low and seductive as he sent her one of his devastating, crooked smiles.

'How?' she whispered on a breathless gasp.

'Wait and see.'

Jen was bursting with curiosity as Camille dashed back into the office. 'Just look at you!'

'I'm only ten minutes late,' Camille said. 'What about me?'

'You've got the afterglow of a woman who's just been—'

'Eating,' Camille supplied quickly. 'I've been eating fish cakes and drinking champagne at Cicero's.'

Jen beamed. 'Another date with the boy from the bush?'

'Yes.' Camille flopped into her chair. 'But don't make anything of it, Jen.'

'Why not? It's not often that sharing something as safe as a meal with a guy makes a woman look the way you do right now.'

Camille dimpled. 'I guess.'

'She guesses,' Jen mimicked. Frowning, she wandered across the room to stand beside Camille's chair. 'Jonno Rivers is more or less perfect, isn't he?'

Camille chewed at her lower lip as she picked up a pen and twisted it between her fingers. 'More or less.'

'Millie, don't tell me you've found faults with the god.'

'No, not faults.'

'You two click, don't you?'

'Oh, yes.' Camille positioned the pen back in the bright red mug on her desk with unnecessary care. 'I guess you could say we click exceptionally well.' Man, just thinking again about last night made her heart gallop and her skin tingle. Jonno was a lover beyond compare.

'So what's the problem?' asked Jen.

'There isn't a problem really.'

'O...K,' Jen said slowly. 'But...?' she supplied with an expectant air.

Camille sighed. 'But I'm scared I'm going to hurt him.'

Jen sank onto the edge of Camille's desk and stared at her. 'Why would you do that?'

'Oh, Jen, I'm hopelessly attracted to him, but I don't think I'm right for him. He's a country boy, with down-on-the-farm wholesome values.'

'Camille, you're not exactly a loose woman.'

Camille winced. Right now that was exactly how she felt.

'You know what your problem is?' Jen said.

'You're going to tell me, aren't you?'

'But it's obvious. Look at the way you've dated ever since I've known you. You go out with guys who are...' She wiggled her hand in a so-so gesture. 'You take enormous care to date guys who are presentable, but who are too safe and predictable to actually make you fall in love.' Jen patted Camille's shoulder. 'This time, honey, you've stepped over that line.'

Camille's jaw dropped as she stared at her friend. 'When did you become so perceptive?'

Jen shrugged and smiled archly. 'I read your series on the A to Z of dating.' Then she leaned closer and slipped a reassuring arm around Camille's shoulders. 'Seriously, Millie, what are you worried about? Do you think that now that Jonno's read your article about marriage in the outback he'll expect you to bury yourself in the bush to produce his babies?'

Camille covered her face with trembling hands. That was exactly what she was worrying about.

'Have you talked to him about this?' Jen asked.

Lowering her hands, Camille met Jen's level gaze. 'No, but I must,' she said with sudden determination. 'He's going home tomorrow, so I'll do it tonight.'

CHAPTER SEVEN

PLAY it cool, man, Jonno told himself as he stood on the front steps of his hotel and watched Camille walking towards him across a busy pedestrian crossing.

Rays from the setting sun slanted down past city skyscrapers to splash auburn tints through her dark hair, and she looked so good in her slim-fitting black top and a short red tartan skirt that she made him think of a rare and colourful wild flower in a paddock of drab weeds.

When she reached him, she rose on tiptoe to kiss his cheek and he smelled her perfume. He felt the brush of her soft skin and the warm pressure of her breasts against his arm, and the force of his need for her was so savage he wanted to howl.

Play it cool. Yeah, right.

'So what's the plan for this evening?' she asked.

He swallowed. 'I was thinking that, as you're such an old hand at ordering Room Service, we could eat in my hotel room tonight.'

'OK,' she said after a momentary hesitation. 'A night in would be nice.'

On the way to the eighth floor they had the lift to themselves, and Jonno couldn't resist drawing her close and kissing her. Nothing brash. Just a sweet hello. An invitation... It drew a surprised little gasp from her and then a soft, glad sound of acceptance as she kissed him back.

Ah, Camille…

All day he'd been tense, wondering if perhaps she wouldn't want him as eagerly as she had last night, but her kiss was warm and needy, and when he closed the door of his hotel room he had only to touch her arm and she was curling against him, her sweet, willing mouth lifted to his.

Camille… Camille…

She shouldn't be kissing Jonno like this.

She was supposed to be resisting him. When she'd left work she'd planned to start the evening with a discussion about where their relationship was heading.

But Jonno was wrecking her plans. Right from the start he'd looked too, too gorgeous as he stood waiting for her with the late-afternoon breeze lifting his hair. And then his mouth had tilted into that funny-sad, sexy smile of his and her good intentions had taken a sideways slip.

Added to that, he had ideas of his own about how this night should be spent. And right now *his* ideas were sending cascades of heat all the way through her. He was holding her wrists above her head and nudging her gently but very deliberately back against the door.

'Jonno,' she said weakly as he held her arms high, but her next words were lost as his gorgeous mouth took hers with warm, potent, slow kisses. Soul-deep kisses.

'I want to fulfil your fantasy,' he murmured. 'But we need a little water.'

Surprise sent her thoughts scattering. 'Water? What are you talking about?'

Keeping hold of her wrists, he lowered them to her sides, stepped back and tugged her away from the door. 'Warm water,' he said. 'A grown-ups' version of a hose fight.'

Oh, man.

His smile was pure pirate as he scooped her into his arms and proceeded to carry her across the room. 'I think you need a shower.'

A shower with Jonno? Seeing Jonno wet and naked? Oh, help! How could she conduct a serious discussion about an uncertain future when she was in Jonno's arms and heading for the shower?

'Not the shower!' she cried, but her exclamation sounded more like the hammed-up terror of a pantomime heroine than a genuine protest.

'Anything but the shower!' Jonno mocked.

And Camille couldn't resist playing along. 'I demand that you unhand me, sir!'

'Unhand you, wench?' In the bathroom doorway he let her down so quickly she fell against him, and before she could step away he was tickling her ribs. 'Shall I unhand you like this?'

'Yes!' she cried, laughing helplessly. 'I mean no! Not tickling!'

With two steps he backed her into the luxurious white and gold bathroom. 'Like this, then?' he murmured, his eyes brimming with laughter as his hands slipped beneath her top and he feathered her ribs with electric caresses.

She tried to say no. She *might* have said no if his eyes hadn't grown dark, if his mouth hadn't descended onto hers and if his hands hadn't slowed till they swept over her skin in hot, possessive figures of eight, inching higher and higher till they reached her breasts.

It was impossible to resist him. His mouth and hands were already making love to her. His hard, masculine body was surging against hers. And how could she keep fighting when it felt so right? Everything about Jonno felt so very right.

But this would have to be the last time…

They ate the meal Camille ordered from Room Service sitting picnic-style on the richly carpeted floor, wrapped in the huge white towelling bathrobes the hotel provided and with their hair still damp from the shower.

They talked about Paris and Jonno told Camille about a fascinating piano bar he'd discovered in Montmartre.

'It just pulses with Parisian atmosphere,' he said. 'You know the sort of thing—low, heavily beamed ceilings papered with old posters, red and white checked table-cloths and the whole place full of cigarette smoke. A pianist in the corner playing something nostalgic. But the best thing is all the fascinating messages pinned to the walls.'

'What kind of messages?'

'Postcards, love letters, drawings, jokes. They're mostly from tourists, so lots are in English…'

'When did you go to Paris?' she asked. 'You certainly soaked up the atmosphere.'

'The first time was when I was twenty-one. I spent

twelve months backpacking around Europe. But I was there last year, too. That's when I found this bar.'

'You've been to Paris *twice*?'

He tried not to feel annoyed by her surprise and the clear implication that she still thought of him as a country hick.

The conversation dwindled a little after that, and Jonno wondered if Camille was feeling the same sense of heaviness that he felt. A weight that was crushing his attempts to remain light-hearted. A darkness that stemmed from uncertainty about where they were heading…about the things they hadn't said. The questions they hadn't asked each other.

When they'd finished eating Camille picked up their empty plates and carried them to the side-table beneath the window.

She stood there for a moment, looking out into the night, and when she turned back to him he thought he could see the brightness of tears in her eyes. She was fiddling nervously with the ties of her robe.

'Jonno,' she said, 'you're going back to Mullinjim tomorrow and we need to talk.'

'Sure.' He rose from the floor and indicated the two armchairs in the corner of the suite.

But Camille didn't move. She remained standing with her back to the window, fiddling with the ties at her waist, and so he stayed where he was in the middle of the room, with his feet planted wide apart and his hands resting solidly on his hips.

'I'm worried that you've got the wrong idea about me,' she said.

He felt a jolt of alarm. 'What idea is that?'

'Oh, Jonno. I don't know how to say this without sounding tarty and shallow, but I don't think we should stay in touch after you go home.'

'Why the hell shouldn't we?'

She used the towelling tie to brush at her eyes. 'I'm not the right woman for you.'

His insides seemed to freeze, but somehow he forced words past the iceberg in his throat. 'What if I think otherwise?'

With an impatient shake of her head she said, 'How can I be suitable?'

'Camille, you're talking rubbish. Come here.'

'No,' she cried, holding her hands out as if to ward him off. 'I'll go to pieces if you touch me. If you start kissing me again I'll forget what I'm trying to say.'

'Doesn't that tell you something about how *suitable* we are for each other?'

'I don't know. I don't think so. What I'm trying to say feels so complicated. I'm sure you know that I'm very, very attracted to you—and I don't think you see me as a quick fling while you're in the city.'

He didn't answer, but waited for her to continue.

'But we live thousands of kilometres apart.'

'Aeroplanes can make short work of that.'

'But all that travelling would only be worthwhile if we thought we had a future.'

'And you don't think we do?' he asked coldly.

'I told you right back when we first met that I don't believe in marriage.'

'Who said anything about marriage? If you don't want it, I don't need marriage.'

She sent him a sharp, worried glance. 'Are you sure, Jonno?'

He sighed heavily and ran an anxious hand back and forth over his nape. 'Are *you* sure you *don't* want marriage?' he asked. 'That article you wrote sounded like a sincere tribute to the joys of an outback marriage.'

She seemed to crumple when he said that. Leaning against the window ledge and keeping her gaze averted, she said, 'I was writing that article for other women, not for me.'

'What the hell does that mean?' He was angry now. Damn angry.

'A journalist shapes her writing to suit the audience. I was saying what our readers want to hear.'

'You mean all that stuff you wrote that so impressed Piper—was all rubbish? Just any old words thrown together for the sake of your magazine's circulation?'

'No.' She looked ill. 'I did mean what I said in the article, Jonno. I was being honest. I believe the kind of marriage I wrote about is a rewarding, fulfilling experience for most women—the ultimate dream. It's just that none of that applies to *me*.'

She took two steps towards him and stopped. 'Oh, this is so hard. I guess what I'm trying to explain is that, while most girls spend their lives searching for Mr Right, I've spent the past ten years terrified that I might find him.'

Jonno's heart plunged. 'Why, Camille? Why are you

so frightened? Is it because of your parents? Has their unhappiness messed you around that much?'

Her pale cheeks grew paler and she looked down at her bare toes. 'Perhaps.'

Under his breath, Jonno swore.

Camille lifted her gaze. 'That's a big part of the reason I want to go to Paris. I need to see my father, to talk to him. Mum refuses to discuss their marriage with me, but Dad and I were good mates when I was little.'

'Then I'd better hurry home and sell those steers so you can get over there.'

She looked as if she tried to smile, but her lips were pressed tightly together, and her eyes shimmered damply. After a moment she said, 'When I get to Paris I'll keep a look-out for that piano bar.'

'Yeah,' he said gruffly. 'You do that.'

As a taxi sped her home to her flat, Camille fought to hold back her tears. Jonno was letting her go. Not just to Paris, but out of his life.

He hadn't tried to make love to her again. He hadn't tried to tease her or make her smile. He hadn't even suggested that they keep in touch by letter or phone. Of course that was what she had asked for, so it was unreasonable of her to be disappointed.

Nevertheless, tears welled in her eyes and pooled in a painful lump in her throat and her mouth trembled and pulled out of shape with the effort of refusing to cry.

She'd been completely successful in her mission. She'd convinced Jonno Rivers that she was a totally screwed-up head case and he was better off without her.

And he was. That was the terrible truth. He needed someone stable and sensible, like Gabe's Piper, someone who embraced the concept of marriage and babies without turning a hair.

She shoved a fist against her mouth to hold back another threatening sob. The most horrible part of it was, she didn't know how on earth she was going to get over him.

How could she bear the thought of never seeing him again?

CHAPTER EIGHT

As soon as Camille crossed the threshold of the café on Rue Gabrielle and saw the low-beamed ceilings, the old posters coated with shellac and the walls covered with hundreds of pieces of paper bearing handwritten messages, she knew she'd found Jonno's piano bar.

She'd spent a chilly November afternoon searching in the streets below Butte de Montmartre, but now that she'd found it she felt a sense of anticlimax as she removed her coat and took a seat at a vacant table. OK, she was here, but what a fruitcake she was.

Instead of following through with her intentions to hit all the really high-profile tourist spots in gay Paris, like climbing the Eiffel Tower, taking a boat down the Seine or visiting the Musée d'Orsay, she was sitting in a bar in a back street because Jonno had sat here.

Feeling blue.

Wishing he was here now.

Perhaps she could blame her low mood on the worry she'd shouldered ever since she'd visited her father. Chances were she'd been even more upset by their reunion than she realised. It had been such a shock to visit his tiny, shabby flat and have her old memories of her strong, handsome, fun-seeking dad forced aside by the reality of the man he'd become.

No wonder his letters had been so infrequent and

brief. Fabrice Devereaux had been hiding from her, hoping she wouldn't discover that he'd become an empty shell of the strong father she remembered.

Unlike her mother, who'd progressed from dancing to becoming a brilliant and highly sought-after choreographer, her dad had drifted from one second-rate dance-teaching post to another, becoming lonelier and lonelier and losing his stamina and his zest for life.

But what really shocked Camille was his regret over the mess he'd made of his marriage...

'I really miss your mother,' he'd said. 'I was crazy to let her go.'

'But if you were making each other miserable...?' she'd suggested tentatively.

'Laine and I both had rarefied artistic temperaments and that never helps any relationship,' he'd admitted. 'But beneath all the flame-throwing there was deep affection.' His eyes had grown damp. 'I don't know how I lost sight of that.'

At the time his words had been a blow, like a stab wound to Camille's heart. How could her father have let himself down so badly? How could he nurse regret all these years and do nothing...? And the more she thought about it, the more she wondered if her mother was lonely, too.

Laine Sullivan worked at a killing pace and Camille had always been proud of her achievements. She'd looked up to her mother as a shining example of what a woman with talent and drive could achieve. But was she working so hard merely to fill the gaps in her life?

Had her parents made a terrible mistake when they separated?

The other problem was that thinking about her parents made her think about Jonno…about how wretched she'd felt ever since she'd broken up with him.

He'd stuck by his word, and the only communication they'd had since Sydney was when he'd sent her the money for her steers.

But had she made a fatal mistake? Was she doomed to spend the rest of her life miserable and lonely like her father? Had she inherited some kind of lack-of-courage gene that held her back from reaching for happiness?

A waiter arrived and she ordered a glass of Beaujolais because it was one French wine she was confident she could pronounce, then she took a deep breath and looked around her.

Now that she'd gone to so much trouble to find this place, she should try to enjoy it.

In the far corner a young man was playing slow, moody blues on a piano, but she was already feeling lonely and sentimental so she turned her attention to the amazing assortment of messages pinned to the grey carpet on the café's walls. Fascinated, she leaned closer.

Amidst the clutter was a faded passport photo signed by Julian of England. Someone else called Elvira had written *'C'est la vie la Paris!'* in purple ink on gold paper. And Tobias of Sweden had sketched a cheeky drawing of a partially clad woman onto a drink coaster.

She was about to examine a postcard from 'Paul et Pascalle', when her mobile phone began to beep, and at that same moment the waiter returned with her glass of wine.

'Thanks— I mean, *merci*,' she said to the waiter as she flung euros onto his tray. Her phone was in the pocket of her coat, which was hanging over the back of her chair, and she fumbled frantically before she found it. 'Hello…I mean, *bonjour*.'

'Is that Camille Devereaux?'

The masculine voice had a nasal Aussie drawl that was wonderfully familiar.

'Jonno?' She drew in a quick, gasping breath. 'How— how are you?'

'I'm fine, thanks. How are you? How's Paris?'

'Paris is—Paris is amazing.' She felt such a rush of joy to be talking to Jonno. Her heart was jumping about in her chest like a startled frog. 'Everything here is so— so…'

'So *French*?' he supplied.

She laughed. 'Oh, yes. Paris is very French. Oh, Jonno, you've no idea how good it is to hear your voice.' As the words left her lips she felt her cheeks flame. She hadn't meant to sound quite so eager. She was supposed to have broken up with him.

But he'd caught her by surprise and she couldn't set her thoughts in order. She'd been feeling so lonely, so conscious of how far from home she was and so sick with concern for her father. So wishing Jonno was here.

But thank heavens he wasn't. She might have thrown herself into his arms and made a fool of herself. At least she could speak to him on the telephone safe in the knowledge that he was on the other side of the world.

She could picture him at the desk in his study at Edenvale.

She felt a pang of homesickness, which was crazy, considering that it was Jonno's home she was picturing, not her own.

He would be sitting at the old oak desk and beside him there would be a pile of stock-market reports in a red folder. Behind him in the corner would be the computer that stored all his business records, and on the wall to his right his map of the paddocks on Edenvale would be displaying his grazing schedule for resting and utilising pasture.

Through the window behind him he would have a view of the sweep of bluegrass running down to the billabong with its black ducks and magpie geese.

'You'll never guess where I am right now,' she said.

'Where?'

'At that piano bar you told me about. The one in Montmartre.'

'Really? What do you think of it?'

'I haven't been here long, but it seems to have a terrific ambience.'

'It has, hasn't it? And have you seen your father, Camille?'

'Yes.'

Jonno was silent, as if he was waiting for her to say more, then he asked, 'How is he?'

She sighed. 'He's terribly sad, Jonno. I was devastated to see how old he looks. He's not very well and he's dreadfully lonely.'

'I'm sorry to hear that.' He sounded genuinely caring

and tears spilled onto her cheeks. Suddenly she felt as lonely as her father, lonely and wishing she could see and touch Jonno.

Oh, how she missed him! Why on earth had she sent him away? She could really do with his solid arm around her shoulders right now.

She had to take a deep breath before she could continue. 'Dad's missing my mother, Jonno. He says he's always missed her. I can't bear to see how lonely he is.'

There was a stretch of silence before he said, 'That's tough.' And he sounded so understanding she had to press three fingers to her lips to hold back a sob. She drew a quick breath. 'I'm trying to talk him into coming back to Australia with me.'

'Good idea. Let me know if there's any way I can help.'

Surprised, Camille sniffed her thanks.

'And what about you?' he asked. 'Have you been having some fun?'

'Yep.'

It was almost the truth. She was *planning* to have fun. She glanced at the wall beside her, crammed with messages from hundreds of people having fun in Paris, the most romantic city in the world. Starting tomorrow, she would definitely have fun. 'I have a whole string of sightseeing trips lined up.'

'You don't sound too excited.'

'I'm—I'm working on it. I...' Her gaze was dragged back to a spot on the wall where her eyes had been caught by a familiar word. Had she seen what she *thought* she'd seen?

For a split-second she fancied she'd read her name on a note there. *'Camille...'* in thick black handwriting. She searched the sea of messages again.

'Camille?' Jonno was saying.

Yes, there it was. *'Camille'.*

So what? Paris was full of Camilles. *Camilles, Moniques, Francines...*

But there was something about the handwriting.

Oh, my God! *Oh, my God!*

'Camille, are you there?'

She was reading the note on the wall.

Camille, I want you. I need you. We can do this any way you like as long as you're mine.

                                        Love, Jonno.

Her heart thrashed, skipped a beat and thrashed some more. She almost dropped the phone.

'Jonno,' she squeaked.

There was no answer.

Her face was on fire and her heart was thumping. She was shaking. Tears streamed down her cheeks.

What was going on? Surely there couldn't be two couples called Jonno and Camille? But how could that message be here? Jonno was at home in the Mullinjim valley on the other side of the globe. Had he sent this note by mail? Had he asked someone to put it there?

She tried the phone again. 'Jonno, are you still there?'

'Yes. I'm here.'

'I think I'm going crazy. There's a note on the wall

in this café to a girl with my name from a guy called Jonno.'

'What's so crazy about that?' She thought she heard a hint of laughter in his voice.

She darted quick glances around the café, searching through the dozens of people who were talking, drinking and smoking for a waiter. Perhaps a waiter could explain how the note had got here. But she couldn't speak French. How silly. What was the use of having a French father when he hadn't taught her his language?

'Camille.' Jonno's voice sounded in her ear. 'Can you see a little red-framed window on the street-side of the café?'

Her eyes flew to it. 'Yes.'

'Have you checked the view from there? It's kind of special.'

What could be so remarkable about the view down a Montmartre back street? Feeling just a little silly, she walked over to the little low window, ducked and peered through it to the street outside.

And almost sank to the floor with shock.

Jonno was standing on the opposite corner, leaning against a lamp post with a familiar, easy nonchalance.

Her face burned and her heart hurled itself against her ribs as she stood staring.

She glanced down at the phone in her shaking hand, then out of the window again.

He was wearing a navy woollen sweater and blue jeans, with a black leather jacket slung over his shoulder, and he looked as at home on a Parisian street corner as he did propped against the stock rails at Edenvale.

He lifted a hand to wave at her.

She gave a little half-wave and, with legs of jelly, made her way to the café's entrance. *Jonno was here in Paris.* Her fingers gripped the lintel and she stood riveted in the doorway. Jonno. Here. In Paris. She wasn't sure if she was laughing or crying.

She felt a rush of confusion, excitement warring with fear. She'd told him to forget about her, so why was he here?

Memories of their nights in Sydney came in an aching, hot flood. Her chest filled with an up-rush of sweet, painful longing as he took long, steady strides down the footpath towards her.

When he drew near, he sent her a cautious smile. One stride away from her, he stopped and stood for a stretch of time, looking at her without speaking. Somehow he seemed taller and more broad-shouldered than ever. More Jonno, if such a thing were possible. *And I must look a teary mess!*

His mouth quirked into a shy smile. 'What can I say but g'day?'

'G'day,' Camille whispered.

She was blocking the doorway and other people were waiting to get in. 'Come inside,' she said quickly.

She had no choice but to lead him back to the table where she'd left her coat and wine glass, and it was a relief to sit down and give her shaking knees a chance to recover. 'What are you doing here? I can't believe it. Who's looking after your cattle?'

'Gabe and Piper,' he said. 'They owe me one or two favours.' His hazel eyes studied her face and he gave a curt nod towards her untouched glass. 'Looks like you could do with some of that wine.'

Like an obedient child she took a deep sip and her hands shook as she set the glass back on the table. 'Are you going to order something?'

'Not yet.'

'I just can't believe you're *here*.'

'I've taken up a new hobby—turning up out of the blue. First Sydney, now Paris.'

Camille's thoughts and feelings rioted and fought for space in her head and she couldn't trust herself to speak. It was so good to see Jonno, but he shouldn't have come. She'd missed him so much, but she had no right to miss him. They'd agreed to a break-up and yet here he was.

With his thumb, Jonno traced the path of a tear on her cheek. 'You might be surprised to know I came here on your advice.'

'My advice?' Her mouth sagged open. 'What do you mean?'

He swallowed and looked suddenly nervous. 'Ages ago you told me that, if you have no alternative, you take a gamble.'

'Oh.'

'I gambled on coming from Mullinjim to Paris to find you.'

'But—but...' Dared she ask this question? 'Why didn't you have any alternative?'

For answer, he leaned across the table and pulled the note from the wall and with strong brown fingers spread it flat on the red and white tablecloth.

She stared at the message with a hand pressed against her thumping heart.

Camille, I want you. I need you. We can do this any way you like as long as you're mine.

Love, Jonno.

'I put one of these notes near every table, hoping to catch your eye,' he said.

'Oh, my goodness.'

'This is why I'm here, Camille. I've come all this way to tell you that I'm not going to let you talk us out of something we both want.'

'But—'

He held up his hand. 'Before you start panicking, hear me out. I'm not asking you for marriage or babies. Just us. You and me.'

'But that's not fair if you want—'

'This note says it all. I want *you*, Camille. If you don't want marriage, that's OK. If you want to stay in Sydney, that's OK, too, but there's not a damn thing that's OK about pretending we shouldn't see each other any more.'

Her hands were tightly clenched on the table in front of her and he reached out and covered them with his big, tanned hand. 'You've no idea how I feel about you. I'd leave Edenvale if it made you happy.'

'Oh, no!' She felt a flash of panic. 'You mustn't do that.' In her eyes Jonno and Edenvale were inseparable. 'I'm not worth it, Jonno.'

For a long block of time he sat there, looking at her,

his hand warm and firm over hers, his gaze sad and speculative. 'One day you're going to understand that you're worth much more.'

Unable to meet the intensity of his gaze, she stared at their entwined hands. It was so hard to believe that this big, gorgeous man wanted her and her alone. Her chest felt so full of emotion she thought it might burst like a flood gate.

Jonno had come all this way to tell her he wanted her on *her* terms with no strings attached. An unconditional relationship.

'Stop fighting this, Camille.'

He lifted his hand away and she grabbed it between trembling fingers.

'I can't believe you've gone to so much trouble to find me.' She thought of her parents, both hiding from each other in different ways. Her father, afraid to admit to her mother how lonely he was. 'I've been miserable without you, Jonno.'

His smile was slow and sweetly one-sided. 'No one should be miserable in Paris.' He stood and, with her hands still in his, drew her to her feet. 'Let's hit this town, Camille. If two Aussies can't make a mark on this city I'll trade in my riding boots.'

They left the café, pulled on their coats to keep out the sudden chill wind and made their way down the streets of Montmartre. The afternoon unfurled like a movie reel throwing up scenes from a favourite, much-loved film.

On a street corner, the tempting aroma of roasting chestnuts lured Jonno and he bought a paper cone-full to share with Camille as they headed for the Metro, which took them back to the heart of Paris.

They traversed the full length of the Champs-Élysées from the Arc de Triomphe to the Louvre, lingering past the glamorous stores selling everything from sports cars and perfume to chocolate and lingerie. They stopped for coffee and crêpes at one of the chic restaurants sporting red canvas awnings and instant gardens made up of potted marigolds.

'Edith told me I'm to take careful note of the Parisian women's fashion flair,' Camille said as they continued down the famous avenue.

'That's preferable to having you check out the French blokes,' Jonno replied. 'They're supposed to be loaded with sex appeal, aren't they?'

'They wish,' she said with a laugh. 'The French guys aren't a patch on you, Jonno Rivers.'

She was rewarded with a kiss. Right there on the Champs-Élysées while hundreds of Parisians hurried past. Nobody seemed to mind. After all, this was Paris. The city of love. Paris in the autumn.

And nobody minded when, moving with lightning speed, Jonno lifted Camille, spun her behind him and ran with her piggyback-style with her arms wrapped around his neck and her legs wound around his waist.

'Put me down!' she gasped between helpless bursts of laughter, but of course he ignored her.

And their laughter trailed behind them as he ran with her down the Champs-Élysées past twin avenues of trees, while autumn leaves danced and spun in the wind, catching light at different angles and flashing their hectic colours like sequins on a ball gown.

Finally, when they were both breathless, panting and helpless, he lowered her feet to the pavement—and kissed her again.

Paris with Jonno was beyond perfect.

In the days that followed, Camille couldn't believe it was possible to be so incredibly happy every minute of the day. And night.

She and Jonno were two people in love, alone together in a world where nobody knew them, and they lived purely on impulse, filling their days spontaneously, without planning. A trip to the markets for baguettes and brie inspired an impromptu picnic in the Jardin du Luxembourg. After visiting art galleries, they felt moved to dine in the Latin Quarter. A night at the theatre seemed to call for a lingering walk home, hand in hand along the lamp-lit banks of the sleepy Seine.

Jonno hired a sports car and they spent a day dashing south from Paris into a patchwork of fields and isolated farmhouses with honey-brown roofs and grey stone walls. They lunched beside a river where dark, silken water slipped from beneath the solid stone arches of an ancient bridge and brushed the garden walls of centuries-old houses before making its way to the shadows of willows and oaks further downstream.

'It's so incredibly different from the Australian outback, isn't it?' said Camille.

Jonno was stretched on the picnic rug, propped on one elbow. He surveyed the scene and sent her a lazy smile.

'I think we've agreed that everything in France is very French.'

Camille laughed and he rolled her close so he could kiss her again.

Back in Paris once more, they lit candles in Notre Dame Cathedral. They kissed at the top of the Eiffel Tower, then rushed home to make love. Again and again.

'I've never been so happy,' Camille told Jonno as she lay in the haven of his arms and looked up to a long, narrow window that offered them a view of bare tree branches and pointed roof tops outlined against a patch of powder-blue morning sky.

'That makes two of us,' he murmured, lowering his lips to drop a warm kiss onto her bare shoulder.

She turned and smiled into his eyes and traced his profile with her finger, delighting in the texture of masculine skin as her fingertip slid down his forehead, between his dark brows to the jut of his nose, over the sensuous swell of his lips to his rough unshaven chin.

'Thank you, Jonno,' she whispered. 'Thank you for wanting me this much.'

Her hand lingered at his chin and he trapped it there in his, then raised her fingers to his mouth and took each tip lightly between his teeth…and nibbled them one by one. 'The appreciation's mutual,' he said, pressing his lips into the palm of her hand, her wrist, the curve of her elbow.

They didn't talk of love, but that was OK. Talking of love led to talk of marriage and commitment and they both knew that wasn't on the agenda. They were a twenty-first-century couple. Right for each other. For now.

She smiled and yawned and stretched beside him like a sleepy cat in the sun, enjoying the vastness and depth of her happiness and the blissful sense of freedom that came with it. And as she stretched her body slid against Jonno's in a long, lazy roll—which they both knew was a prelude to more lovemaking.

But the moment was spoiled by the beeping of his mobile phone on the bedside table.

He glanced at the clock. 'That'll be Piper ringing with an update.'

Kissing her quickly, he reached over to pick up the phone and Camille lay back against the pillow and enjoyed the view of his long, tanned back. Masculine muscles, honed by years of hard work, rippled beneath coppery skin.

Lost in her secret admiration, she paid little attention to his conversation, until it occurred to her that he was saying very little and that his hand was gripping the phone so tightly his knuckles were white. She heard him curse softly and next moment he swung clear away from her, sitting up straight with his legs over the edge of the bed. There was more silence as he listened intently to the caller. And then, 'No. No! Hell, no!'

Alarm snaked through Camille, quickly followed by guilt. She felt like an eavesdropper overhearing an important personal call. Should she stay here beside Jonno or would he feel freer to talk if she left?

Slipping out of bed, she walked around its foot, pausing for a moment beside him in case he showed any sign of needing her presence. But he didn't look up. She counted to twenty as she waited, but he gripped the phone against his ear. She counted on to forty, but Jonno continued to stare at the floor and didn't seem to be aware of her.

With such clear evidence that this call had nothing to do with her, she walked purposefully through to the *en suite* bathroom and closed the door behind her.

CHAPTER NINE

As CAMILLE showered, she expected Jonno to finish his phone call and come to her. When he didn't, she dried herself quickly, shoved her arms into the sleeves of a bathrobe and tugged it around her as she hurried back into the bedroom.

He was gone.

A quick check of the room told her he'd thrown on clothes from the day before and left. Left without a word.

She felt suddenly scared. What had happened? He must have gone away to do something urgent. But why hadn't he called out to tell her where he was going?

Her mind raced. Sick waves of panic swooped over her. Something was seriously wrong. Now she regretted leaving Jonno to deal with the call on his own.

But she hadn't wanted to invade his privacy.

And he hadn't wanted to share his news with her. If he had, he would have come into the bathroom to find her.

She sank into a chair and stared at the rumpled bed sheets, still warm from their bodies. Why had he disappeared without a word?

Was this what happened to lovers who didn't speak of love, who only shared each other's passion, went out of their way to avoid making any lasting claims on each other's lives?

They had fun. They had superior sex. But when something serious happened, like this phone call, they simply walked away from each other.

No. No, that couldn't happen to Jonno and her. They had something very special. She was letting her imagination run away. They would be OK.

But she had no idea where he might be, so she couldn't go searching. Feeling wretched, she dressed in pale grey Capri trousers and a dark red sweater he particularly liked, then made instant coffee with the complimentary sachets provided by the hotel and let it grow cold while she waited for him to come back.

When at last she heard Jonno's key in the door, she leapt out of her seat and hurried forward.

He looked pale and drawn and his gaze darted restlessly around the room as if he couldn't look her in the eye. Her heart thudded hollowly as she stood waiting for him to speak. When he didn't she drew a sharp breath and stepped towards him.

'Please, Jonno, I can't bear not knowing. Has something happened to Gabe or Piper, or their children?'

'No,' he said wearily. 'No, they're OK.' His troubled eyes rested on her briefly, then flicked to his suitcase.

She wished she didn't feel so nervous and useless. 'Would you… Shall I ring for fresh coffee and something to eat?'

His lips curved in a faint smile that didn't reach his haunted eyes. 'Where would we be without your Room-Service skills? Yeah, coffee would be good.'

While she dialled and placed their order, he continued to stand in the middle of the room with one hand shoved deep in his jeans pocket and the other scraping restlessly back and forth over the back of his neck.

When she replaced the receiver he said, 'As you've probably guessed, I've had bad news.' He let out a ragged sigh. 'There's been an accident. A tragedy. People back home have been killed.'

'Oh, how awful!'

'But that's not all.' He cleared his throat. 'It appears that I'm a father. I've just been told that I have a son.'

The words hit her like a blast from a furnace. Her cheeks felt scalded. She couldn't breathe. She certainly couldn't speak. And Jonno couldn't meet her gaze, but stood staring at the pattern of pale roses in the carpet at his feet.

'This girl I used to go out with—Suzanne Heath,' he went on in a flat, toneless voice. 'We had an unhappy relationship that dragged on longer than it should have. Anyhow, she became pregnant, but she insisted that another bloke, Charles Kilgour, was the father.'

Camille nodded. This was the woman Piper had told her about. At one stage Jonno had hoped that her baby was his.

'Suzanne ran off with Kilgour,' he said. 'Eventually they married and settled on his property a couple of hundred kilometres away, over near Wattle Park. But—' He paused, dragged in a rough breath and brushed his arm over his eyes '—now Suzanne and Charles have been killed.'

'Oh, no.' The choked cry broke from her lips, but she couldn't move. She felt as if she'd been turned to stone.

Jonno slammed one fist into the palm of his other hand. 'Drink-driving, apparently. They were on their way home from an all-night party.' He let his breath out in a hiss between clenched teeth. 'The little bloke, their—the son wasn't with them. He stayed behind at Wattle Park, with Kilgour's family.'

He paused again and Camille saw his Adam's apple slide up and down in his throat as his bleak gaze swung around to lock momentarily with hers then sheer away again. 'Since the accident the Kilgours are refusing to look after the boy and they're claiming that he's mine.'

She still didn't know what to say. Couldn't think what was right. 'What a...shock...for you.'

He nodded and grimaced, closing his eyes as if he was fighting a dark, forceful emotion. As he opened them again, a knock sounded at the door.

'That'll be our breakfast,' she said.

She opened the door, took the tray and set it on the coffee-table, then poured fragrant hot coffee into two cups and held one out to Jonno.

'Sit down and drink this.'

He took it, muttered his thanks and lowered himself into a chair.

Camille placed a plate with a jam-filled croissant in front of him and then perched on another chair near by and they sipped their coffee in silence. After several minutes she said, 'Do you think the little boy is really your son?'

He looked at her sadly for a heart-stopping moment,

then dropped his gaze to the carpet again. 'It's quite possible. At the time, when I found out Suzanne was pregnant, I thought there was every chance. I didn't know she was two-timing me with Kilgour, of course.'

'Have you ever seen the little boy?'

'No, never.'

Seconds limped by as they sat in painful silence. There were so many questions Camille wanted to ask. Was Jonno mourning Suzanne?

'How old is he?'

He turned to look at her with dazed, empty eyes. 'Two. Around two and a half, I should think.'

'I'm sorry to ask so many questions, but I'm just trying to take it in,' Camille said. 'I don't understand why the Kilgours are saying he's yours now. After all this time.'

'From what my mother tells me, it seems that they were prepared to overlook the fact that the boy looked nothing like Charles, but since—since the accident, they don't want him.'

'How can they just not want him?' she asked, shocked.

'You don't know the Kilgours.'

'Do you know if—if he looks like you?'

'Apparently he does. To start with he has black hair, and Suzanne and Charles both come from fair-haired families.'

Putting his coffee-cup aside, he sat leaning forward with his elbows resting on his knees and his hands hanging limply. 'I can't help wondering how Suzanne felt when the baby was born.'

'She must have had a nasty shock. Was she already married to the other fellow?'

'Yes, they were married, but she wouldn't have admitted her mistake. The Kilgour family promote themselves as the nearest thing to landed gentry in the outback and she'd set her sights on climbing the social ladder.'

He shook his head slowly as he sat staring at the floor. 'But Charles Kilgour was no fool. He would have known the truth. I guess his ego must have prevented him from admitting that the child wasn't his.'

'It's still amazing that they hid the truth from you all this time.'

Jonno nodded silently.

'What's the boy's name?' Camille asked suddenly. For some reason she needed to know, as if this nightmare would make more sense if the child had a name.

'Peter,' he said.

'That's nice.'

'Yeah.'

'Will you ask for a DNA test?'

'I don't really see the point of proving paternity.' His jaw jutted with almost warlike menace. 'Whether this little guy is my biological child or not, he very easily *could* have been, so I still feel as if I share responsibility for him. And if no one else wants him, I sure as hell do. I'm not going to leave him for the state to care for.'

'No,' she whispered. 'You couldn't do that. I can see how you feel.'

Suddenly he jumped to his feet.

'Do you, Camille? Do you understand?'

She pressed her folded arms close to her chest as a wave of fear eddied through her. This scenario was something so far outside her experience, she felt a vast distance opening between herself and Jonno.

'I'm trying,' she said, swallowing back a threat of tears. The last thing she wanted was to cry and make this harder for Jonno. 'I think I can understand what you're going through.'

He began to pace the room again. 'I keep thinking about what I've missed. When Peter was born—all the milestones. I've been watching Gabe's kids grow up and all this time there's been this little guy...'

He grimaced and Camille almost sobbed at the pain in his face. 'And the hell of it is what I've done to you,' he cried. 'What this means for us.'

'Us? Jonno, what are you saying?' Her stomach gave a panicky leap.

'I got so carried away. I charged over here and foisted myself on you.'

She tried to crack a smile. 'Have you heard me complaining?'

He hurried across the room to her, bent low and clasped her face in his hands. His eyes were dark with pain, but he smiled his beautiful, crooked smile as he murmured, 'It's been sensational, hasn't it, sweetheart?'

'Absolutely.' He was talking as if they were past tense. She could hardly breathe she felt so scared. Surely this little boy didn't mean that it was all over between them?

Swinging quickly upright again, Jonno groaned. 'I thought I was a free agent, Camille, but the no-strings relationship I proposed is a joke now. I thought I could turn up here and make everything right. I was willing to give up Edenvale for you.'

Oh, God. He was assuming that because he'd acquired a son and heir she would run a mile. Could she blame him? After everything she'd said about not wanting marriage…or children?

It was true she'd never thought of herself as the motherly type, but if it meant losing Jonno…?

He shot her a sharp, warning glance. 'I've booked my flight back.'

'Already?' she cried. 'Do you have to go so soon?'

'Yes, I went straight to the travel agency down the road. It's bad enough that this poor little fellow has lost his parents. But if nobody wants him— Hell! I've got to get back as soon as I can.'

Sick and empty, Camille stared at him. Jonno was going home. Without her. In his mind, he had already left. She could sense the distance between them as clearly as if he were on the plane and halfway home already.

How could this happen so quickly? One minute she was happier than she'd ever been in her life, or had ever hoped to be, the next everything was gone.

She was losing Jonno.

'I could come with you,' she said.

He kept his face averted. 'It might be best if you don't.'

His untouched croissant was still lying on the plate as he crossed to his suitcase and began to fill it with clothes from the wardrobe.

The next few hours were horrible.

Camille stumbled around their suite, trying to be helpful, ironing him a shirt for the journey, running out to buy him a fresh tube of toothpaste and checking for stray socks under the bed.

She could only remember one other time when she'd felt this scared and miserable. Her mother had been in hospital for emergency surgery and Camille had paced the hospital corridors, terrified that she'd never see Laine again. She'd been suddenly aware of how much she loved her mother, but how inadequate she'd been in expressing that love.

Now she wanted to tell Jonno she loved him. Because she did. She knew that now. Had known it for ages really.

She stood in a corner of the hotel room and stared past the leafless trees down into the grey streetscape below and tried to find the right way to explain to him how she felt.

Her feelings had been evolving since the first time she'd met Jonno, when she thought she'd merely wanted him in her magazine. And then she'd been swept away by his overwhelming charms and she'd wanted him in her bed. But now? Now that she'd lived with him and knew him so well... Oh, heavens, she had a terrible feeling that just getting through a day...facing one block of twenty-four hours after the next...would be impossible without him.

She was dying from the inside out at the thought of losing him.

But since his mother's phone call there was a dis-

tanced remoteness about him that stopped her from trying to give voice to her feelings. She had the impression
that if she suddenly spoke of love Jonno would react
with bitter scorn.

What pathetic timing to discover now, too late, just
how deeply and helplessly in love she was.

And time was rushing away so quickly. How could
she have guessed that her last hours, her final precious
minutes with Jonno, would be spent watching him make
long-distance phone calls to solicitors and to his mother
or helping him to pack. No kisses or cuddles and hardly
any conversation.

They exchanged a handful of words as they travelled
by taxi to Charles de Gaulle Airport.

At the customs barrier Jonno drew Camille close just
once, and she felt his big frame shake as he crushed her
hard against his chest. She heard the savage pounding
of his heart and she couldn't hold back the tears. She
prayed that he wouldn't say something too final—such
as he'd never forget her.

'I'll never forget you,' he whispered, and she saw a
shimmer of silver in his eyes.

She wanted to howl. She wanted to throw herself
down on the airport floor and weep and weep and weep.

His goodbye kiss was a brief brush of his lips against
hers and then he was walking away from her.

Sniffling and battling with tears, she remembered
something she'd meant to give him earlier. She plunged
her hand into her coat pocket and pulled out a small
china French poodle, hot pink with a blue woollen pom-

pom tail. 'I was going to take this back for Bella,' she said, holding it out to him. 'Can you give it to her?'

'Sure.' The tiny ornament looked lost in his big, work-rough hand.

'I'm afraid I don't have anything suitable for a two-year-old boy,' she said, 'but you might like to look in the duty-free shops for some kind of toy to take with you for Peter.'

'That's a good idea. Thanks.' He stared at the little poodle in his hand and then back at her, and she saw a chilling shadow of agony in his eyes as if he was being overtaken by a terrible regret. Then he squared his shoulders and, still holding the poodle, he walked away from her and disappeared, swallowed up by the queue of happy travellers.

As if she needed to punish herself and make herself as miserable as possible, Camille went back to Montmartre—to Jonno's piano bar. And she found all his notes still pinned to the walls. With tears coursing down her cheeks she ignored curious stares as she pulled the notes down and shoved them into her pocket.

Outside again she found a park bench and sat alone, surrounded by a carpet of dead and dying autumn leaves, and she read the notes. Each message was the same, but she read them all.

Camille, I want you. I need you. We can do this any way you like as long as you're mine.

Love, Jonno.

Over and over he'd written those same heartbreaking words. He'd been prepared to do so much for her. *Any way she liked.*

He'd been prepared to change his whole life for her.

Oh, heavens! How easy it had seemed then.

And how selfish she felt now.

If she hadn't made such a fuss about not wanting marriage, if she'd made a commitment to Jonno, if she had been his *wife*, she could have helped him now. Without question he would have turned to her for support. She'd be on the plane with him, standing by him through whatever problems came their way.

But when this terrible news had come he hadn't felt entitled to ask anything of her. He'd stood by his offer of a commitment-free relationship. And he was leaving her so he could face his problems alone.

And she'd never felt so abandoned, so lonely. So unnecessary.

But what do I have to offer Jonno? He knows how hopeless I am with children.

She thought of Piper's children—Bella and Michael—and frowned as she remembered the morning laughs she'd shared with Bella and the way little Michael had snuggled into her like a warm and cuddly koala. At the time she'd been surprised at how much she'd enjoyed them both. She hadn't even minded getting up in the middle of the night to give Michael another bottle.

But perhaps she'd coped so well then because Piper's children were special.

Jonno's child would be special...

A little boy. Only two years old. With dark hair. A

little boy called Peter who would grow up on Edenvale. With his father. He would call Jonno Daddy.

A little boy who needed Jonno—needed the man who had wanted her so much he'd come to Paris to claim her. But that man had left her again to go home to claim his son.

And it was her fault she was alone because she'd never been brave enough to face up to the truth.

CHAPTER TEN

HIS son.

When Jonno walked into his mother's house and saw the little dark-haired, hazel-eyed boy sitting on the mat in front of the television, he felt a stab of painful recognition. The child could have been himself or Gabe as a tiny tot.

His mind zapped straight back to his childhood, to memories of his father playing with him and Gabe, teaching them to ride, to fish, to swim in Mullinjim Creek.

And now he had a son. Out of the blue, this little boy was his. His own flesh and blood. A cousin for Bella and Michael.

'The poor little fellow's had a tough time,' his mother told him. 'From what I've gathered Suzanne and Charles put most of their energy into their social lives and the elder Kilgours were reluctant babysitters. It's going to take a lot of patience and love to win your little boy around, son.'

It broke Jonno's heart to think that his boy might have suffered neglect and lived in a loveless household. And he was damn angry over the way his rights as a father had been ignored, but there was nothing to be gained from dredging up a sense of injustice now.

161

Just as there was nothing to be gained from thinking about Camille.

And how he missed her, how he ached for her.

Now he was back in Mullinjim he had to accept that a relationship without ties was a luxury he could no longer contemplate.

'I want to take Peter straight back to Edenvale,' he told his mother. He was keen to make up for any omissions in his son's life over the past two years. He would do his damn best to show his boy the father's love he deserved.

But on the journey home the boy sat stiffly behind his seat belt, clutching the kangaroo Jonno had bought at the Duty Free in Sydney, not looking to left or right and not saying a word.

When they reached Edenvale Jonno took him into the kitchen, and Peter sat huddled on a chair looking lost and eyeing his strange new father with such terror Jonno might well have been Darth Vader.

Sighing deeply, he scratched his head. He'd thought he was experienced with children. He'd babysat for Piper and Gabe's pair enough times to fancy himself as something of a hit with youngsters.

But this boy was a totally different kettle of fish from his cheeky, show-off niece.

'Would you like a drink of water?' he asked.

Peter shook his head.

'Milk? Juice?'

More head-shaking.

Getting desperate, he offered lemonade, and was rewarded by the tiniest of nods. He handed the boy a tumbler and he took a few sips. A tiny breakthrough! But could a two-year-old live on lemonade?

'I'll cook you Bella's favourite meal,' Jonno said. 'Grilled fish fingers with oven-fried crinkly chips.'

But when he served them up Peter didn't seem interested. He wouldn't even nibble one chip!

'Do you want to watch television?' Jonno asked, but was grateful when the boy shook his head as he realised that there were no children's programmes on at this hour.

Megs, the cat, prowled into the kitchen, looking for her dinner, and Peter watched her with large, solemn eyes. Jonno picked her up and carried her over to the chair. 'Would you like to pat the cat?' he asked. 'She's very soft and she purrs when you pat her.'

But the boy shook his head without speaking and he clutched his kangaroo more tightly than ever.

I was mad to reject Piper's offer of help, Jonno thought, but I wanted to do this alone.

'Too many new faces at once will confuse the boy,' he'd told his well-meaning sister-in-law.

'But you've hardly had time to recover from your long flight and you have a property to run,' Piper had counter-argued. 'You'll have to get someone to help you look after Peter. You can't expect your cleaning lady to double up as a nanny.'

'I know I'll need help,' he'd said, 'but at the start I want to take things very quietly. No extra people and no fuss.'

'He's a little boy not a poddy calf,' Piper replied gently. 'Little humans are different animals with different needs.'

Now Jonno felt the first stirrings of panic. He was running out of bright ideas.

What kind of a father was he?

I'll try the pig thing. Bella loves that. But if that doesn't work I'm a total wipe-out with my own son.

Dropping to his hands and knees, he crawled towards Peter, grinning madly. 'Oink, oink,' he grunted and gently headbutted the boy's stomach while he made piggy noises in the snuffling voice that always made Bella laugh and squeal with delight.

But Peter cried and squealed with terror.

'Sorry, little mate,' Jonno cried, sick to the stomach. He gave the boy's head a tentative pat. 'Don't cry. I didn't mean to frighten you.'

His throat was tight with despair as he paced the room, his mind racing to think of something else, anything else that had worked with Bella and Michael. Perhaps he should jump in the truck and take the boy over to Windaroo and let Gabe and Piper work their magic?

Better to let his pride take a beating than to let his son go on suffering.

He looked through the window above the sink towards his parked truck and saw car lights bobbing along the track that led to the homestead. With a wave of relief, he recognised the outline of Piper's ute.

Good old Piper. In spite of his brush-offs she'd come to lend a hand. What a trooper. She would know how to cheer the poor kid.

Quickly he filled the kettle and set it to boil as he heard the car door slam in the yard.

'Everything will be OK, mate,' he told Peter. 'Your auntie Piper's coming. You'll like her.'

He heard her light step on the stairs leading to the back veranda and poured boiling water into the teapot, grabbed two mugs from the pine dresser.

'Good timing, Piper,' he called. 'Come on in. The back door's a little stiff but just give it a shove.'

He heard the squeak of the door as she pushed it open and then her footsteps coming down the passage to the kitchen.

'You're just what the doctor ordered,' he called.

'That's good.'

Jonno's head jerked up. The voice wasn't Piper's.

'Camille!'

CHAPTER ELEVEN

CAMILLE took a step into the room and stopped. 'Hi, Jonno.'

His mouth dropped open. 'Not you.'

Her heart plummeted through the floorboards.

Not you?

How could Jonno say that? How could he scowl at her so fiercely? After she'd flown all this way to be with him, to help him, how could he dismiss her with two words?

She'd been expecting him to rush forward, to pull her into his arms, to kiss and hug her hard and exclaim how delighted and relieved he was that she'd come after all. Not this scowling, angry beast.

Not 'not you'.

She struggled to breathe, tried to draw in burning breaths, but she couldn't stop the rising panic, couldn't stop her knees from shaking and her lips from trembling.

Surely *not you* had to be the two most horrible words in the English language?

Her gaze flew to the little boy huddled on the chair and the untouched plate of food on the table in front of him. Peter looked so incredibly tiny. He was clutching a toy kangaroo in a death grip.

Oh, God. He was so cute—like a miniature version of Jonno—but he was staring up at her with big, unhappy eyes and he looked as if he'd been crying. Clearly things weren't going well.

'What are you doing here?' Jonno growled.

His eyes narrowed as he took a position behind the boy, his hands gripping the top rung of the chair's ladder back. This was the Jonno she'd first met. The stubborn cattleman who'd refused to co-operate with *Girl Talk*.

She felt too exhausted and numb with shock to answer his question with anything except the simple truth. 'I wanted to help, Jonno.'

His face wore a contemptuous look that almost sent her ducking for cover.

'Perhaps I should have w-warned you I was coming, but I—I jumped on a plane only a couple of hours after you left. I had to come via Tokyo, with an eight-hour stopover there, and then I landed in Cairns. I got a bus— and when I reached Mullinjim Piper lent me her ute.'

'Piper should have known better,' he said. 'She shouldn't have sent you over here.'

Closing her eyes for a second or two, she tried to gather some strength by hunting for excuses for Jonno's behaviour. No doubt he was as tired as she was, and he'd come home to a very tricky situation. Her arrival had thrown him and he'd chosen fight mode as the best line of defence.

Piper had warned her. 'Jonno wants to do this on his own,' she'd said. 'He says he doesn't want help, but I'm sure you can change his mind, Camille.'

Perhaps not.

Jonno cleared his throat. 'I've got a tough situation here and I think it would be better if you drove straight back to Windaroo this evening. Gabe and Piper will put you up.'

For a moment she feared she might collapse at his feet. Heavens, less than forty-eight hours ago she and Jonno had been the world's happiest lovers. They'd been totally one. Body and soul.

And from the moment she'd heard that he had a son she'd felt a kind of pang in her heart. Until then she'd never given much thought to being a mother, and certainly not to mothering another woman's child. But ever since it had been all she could think about.

She'd been desperate to join him, to help him. The last thing she'd expected was to be tossed aside like a used sweet wrapper. If only she could sink through the floorboards.

If she hadn't been so exhausted she might have put up a fight, but she had no energy left for battling with him tonight, so she turned towards the door. 'Goodbye, then, Jonno, and good luck,' she said in a flat, tired voice, but she couldn't bear to look at him. 'I'll be at Windaroo if you change your mind.'

He didn't answer, and she couldn't help turning back for one last glance over her shoulder. A movement caught her eye. Little Peter was getting off the chair.

As she watched, he climbed down and stood looking directly up at her. Camille's heartbeats seemed to grow still, then to take off like a racehorse at a starting gate.

Without meeting Jonno's eyes, she said in her gentlest voice, 'Hello, Peter.'

He continued to stand beside the chair, clutching his

kangaroo and staring at her. His eyes grew bigger, but he didn't look frightened. He began to walk towards her.

She flashed one nervous glance Jonno's way and saw that he looked grey and stricken.

'Where's my mummy?' Peter asked.

Oh, God! The little boy's eyes were so big and hopeful her heart seemed to fill her throat. She dropped to her knees beside him.

Where was his mummy? What could she say? How did anyone answer such a question from a two-year-old? Should she try?

She glanced once more towards Jonno and he was looking almost as forlorn and lost as the little boy. She made a hasty decision to ignore his earlier rejection and follow her heart.

'I like your kangaroo,' she said to Peter, and she lifted one hand very slowly and patted the soft, furry toy.

There was no interruption from Jonno.

Peter's eyes followed her movements and she fancied that he was relaxing slightly. She lifted her hand from the toy and touched his cheek with the backs of two fingers, just a whisper-soft caress. Her breath caught as his head drooped sideways as if he was leaning in to her touch.

She was working purely on instinct now. All she could draw on were the times in her life when she'd felt totally alone and utterly miserable. At times like that there had only been one thing she'd wanted.

'Would you like a cuddle?' she whispered.

At first the boy didn't answer. He stood there staring at her, but then he whispered back, 'Yes. Cuddle.'

Taking a deep breath, she gathered the little sweetheart into her arms and he curled against her chest and let her hold him. Over his head her tear-filled eyes met Jonno's.

When she saw an answering sheen in his eyes she almost sobbed aloud. She was asking for his approval, and although he looked wretched he gave a slight nod, so she picked the boy up and settled herself into a rocking chair in a corner of the kitchen.

Peter curled on her lap with his warm little head resting on her shoulder and, with a grimly compressed mouth, Jonno turned to clear away the untouched fish fingers and chips.

'Your kangaroo seems very tense,' Camille said to the boy. 'Do you think he'd like a massage?'

He didn't answer, but he watched as she stroked and massaged the soft toy's furry tail and legs.

'That's better,' she said. 'Now Kanga's starting to relax. What about you, Peter? Would you like me to do that to you?'

He gave the tiniest of nods, and very gently she worked the tense little muscles in his shoulders and arms. After a while he was much more relaxed. She rubbed his back slowly and then hugged him close, and eventually she felt his body grow heavy and the kangaroo slipped out of his grasp.

'He's asleep.' Jonno's voice came from across the room. He wasn't smiling. 'I've made a pot of tea,' he said. 'Would you like a cup?'

'Thanks,' she said, but her voice was barely above a whisper. The long, anxious and sleepless journey had taken its toll, and suddenly her exhaustion was catching up with her.

She was dimly aware of Jonno doing things with a teapot and mugs, but Peter's relaxation seemed to be seeping into her. She knew there were things she should explain to Jonno, and she tried to organise her thoughts into some kind of order. Where should she start? But it was so hard to think when she was feeling so tired...

Jonno stood holding the mug of tea and looking down at Camille as she slept with his son in her arms. He tried to swallow, but his throat felt as if a hot coal was wedged there.

She shouldn't have come.

Damn it. If he'd wanted a woman to help with Peter tonight he could have asked Piper or his mother. Unlike Camille, Piper and Eleanor Rivers would both be around for the long haul, and they could offer the boy stability. All children needed stability, but his son needed it more than most.

All Camille could offer his son was this brief, token cuddle.

Her head fell sideways and her hair hung in a glossy tumble of dark curls. Oh, hell. He knew the silky feel of those curls as they coiled around his fingers. He knew how soft her skin felt and how sweet it tasted.

The skin at the base of her throat had turned pink from the pressure of the boy's warm head. Two days ago his own head had rested there, his mouth had explored there. Just looking at her now as she slept made him want to lose himself in her.

Jerking his gaze from the perfect picture she made

with his son in her arms, he looked out through the window to where gum trees stretched white, ghostly arms up to the black night sky. Walking away from Camille at the airport in Paris had been the hardest, the *worst* ordeal of his life.

But the thing to remember was why he'd done it. Why he'd walked clear away. He'd promised her a relationship free of ties and he couldn't expect her to change.

So he'd come home to face his responsibility. Alone.

Damn it. She should have left him to get on with this alone. Turning up at Edenvale now could only complicate an already complex problem. Why couldn't she have stayed in the city?

It was bright daylight when Camille woke.

She lay blinking at the strong sunshine as it streamed through the bedroom windows and struggled to remember where she was. Light in Paris was much softer, more muted, and in late November the Parisian air was delightfully cool and crisp. The brightness and the dry heat told her she was in Australia.

Outside a kookaburra laughed and everything fell into place in a rush. The flights...the drive west from the coast...coming to Edenvale...little Peter...Jonno...

She couldn't remember coming to bed. Had she stumbled in here half asleep or had Jonno carried her? Who'd removed her dress and shoes and left her to sleep in this T-shirt? Whose bed was this?

She looked around. The only personal items in the room were the paperback novels in the small bookcase in the corner, so she knew this wasn't Jonno's room. It was the neat, tidy kind of bedroom that was often set aside for guests.

Actually, now that she looked more closely, she remembered that she'd slept here once before. That time the cat had slept on her feet and little Bella had come to visit her in the morning.

So she hadn't slept with Jonno. Suddenly she remembered why. A cold wave of dread washed over her as she recalled how he'd looked and behaved when she'd turned up last night. Stomach clenching, she threw the sheet aside and sat up quickly. She had to find him, had to explain.

She hurried into the kitchen and came to an abrupt halt when she realised that the only signs of human presence were breakfast dishes left in the sink. Where were Jonno and Peter? A quick check of the entire house told her it was empty, and when she peered through several windows towards the stock yards and the home paddocks she saw no signs of life apart from cattle.

A solitary magpie warbled in a gum tree, but the rest of the world was silent. She tried hard not to panic and took some comfort from the fact that Jonno's truck was parked beneath the old tamarind tree. It meant that he had to be on the property somewhere. But where was little Peter? Where had Jonno taken him?

Were they hiding from her?

That's paranoid, Camille. Grow up. She took a deep breath. *Don't panic.* Yesterday when she'd told Piper her plans, Jonno's sister-in-law had been confident that Camille would win him round. She clung to that hope for now.

Helping herself to a towel from the linen cupboard, she showered and changed into clean clothes, then went into the kitchen, made herself some coffee and washed the dirty dishes in the sink.

Several times she went outside to scan the surrounding paddocks, but there was still no sign of Jonno. She couldn't even see the cat or his dog, Saxon—just a few black ducks on the billabong and mobs of cattle scattered here and there, and endless paddocks of summer-dry grass and, above, a parched blue sky.

Inside the house once more, she made a quick reconnoitre of the refrigerator and found eggs, milk, cheese and bacon, so decided to make a quiche. Anything to keep herself busy.

It was strangely comforting to be working in the Edenvale kitchen again. Her last visit had been brief and yet everything seemed so familiar—the old pine dresser with its red and white china, the food bowls for the dog and cat on the floor in the corner, the little carved shelf beside the stove where the tea, coffee and sugar were stored in ceramic canisters.

She knew exactly where Jonno kept a huge bag of flour, at the back of the pantry, and where the sharp knives and the chopping board were stored.

Unfortunately her nerves forced her to work with efficient haste, and all too soon the quiche was in the oven and she'd washed the new lot of dishes.

And she was still waiting.

'I think I'll ring Piper before I go mad,' she said aloud to the empty house. Piper would give her some friendly, down-to-earth reassurance and Camille needed a truck-load of reassurance right now.

She decided to use the phone in the study, but she'd only made it halfway down the hall when she heard the click-click-click of a dog's paws on the timber floor behind her.

'Saxon?'

Jonno's golden Labrador was in the kitchen doorway, panting and wagging his tail.

'Hi, boy!' she cried, running down the hall to meet him. She knelt to rub the top of his golden head between his ears and he gave a happy little yap and licked her cheek and she couldn't believe she was feeling so overjoyed to see a dog. 'Where's Jonno?'

There was a sound in the yard and she looked outside and saw Jonno dismounting from a tall, dark horse. Her heart ballooned with a rush of longing. He looked so gorgeous and so, so familiar. Her man.

Pinning on a smile which she hoped didn't look too forced or wistful, she descended the back steps. 'Hi, there.'

Jonno nodded in her direction, then reached up to lift Peter down from the saddle, and she watched the muscles in his strong arms and remembered the loving welcome she'd always found in his embrace. She knew this man intimately. She'd learned by heart every exquisite detail of his long, rangy body. With him she'd shared her all. Together they'd experienced the shattering force of deep, soul-meets-soul passion.

But now he seemed as distant as the Snowy

Mountains. It tore her apart to see how quickly he'd turned into this grim, remote stranger.

But the little boy's eyes were shining and his cheeks were flushed and he looked a hundred times happier than he had last night.

'You two look as if you've been having fun,' she called, and she began to walk towards them.

'We have,' Jonno said over his shoulder while he tied the horse's reins to a fence post. 'I've been showing Pete his new home.'

'What a great idea.'

'And now we're hungry,' he said as she reached them. 'We're starving, aren't we, little mate?'

'I thought you might be hungry. I have a quiche in the oven.'

Jonno looked at her strangely. 'You shouldn't have gone to so much trouble.'

'Oh, it wasn't any trouble.' Good grief, now she felt like a try-hard loser. An impostor. 'I was at a loose end...' She shrugged and left her sentence unfinished. This felt so bad. Jonno was still tense with her. He didn't seem to understand why she'd come.

Couldn't he guess?

Peter looked down from the safety of Jonno's arms with steady hazel-green eyes. Jonno's eyes. 'Camille,' he said.

She drew in a sharp breath. 'Yes,' she said. 'That's my name. I'm Camille.'

She shot Jonno a curious glance and he looked uncomfortable and shrugged. 'He wanted to know what your name was. Actually, to be exact, he asked what the

pretty lady's name was.' His face was expressionless as
he set Peter on the ground.

To Camille's surprise, the boy wanted to walk back
to the house between them, with a hand in each of theirs.

Like a proper little family, she thought.

'So he's opened up?' she asked quietly as they headed
up to the homestead.

'Well, he was happy enough to come riding with me,
but he's mainly been asking about you.'

It was a grudging admission and Camille wished
Jonno didn't have to look so displeased. 'Taking him for
a horse ride was a stroke of brilliance,' she said warmly.

'It's the only thing I've got right so far.'

'But it's not surprising your son likes riding. You
Rivers men were practically born in the saddle, weren't
you?'

His eyes flashed her a quick look of gratitude but then,
as if he regretted the weakness, he hid it beneath another
frown.

When they reached the house, she asked Peter, 'What
would you like for lunch?'

'Dynamite,' he said solemnly.

'Dynamite?' She glanced towards Jonno, but he
looked as puzzled as she was.

'Dynamite bread,' the boy said.

'Beats me,' Jonno said, scratching his head. 'Sounds
tricky.'

'I wonder if he means Vegemite?' Camille suggested.
'Vegemite sandwiches.' She hunted in the pantry cupboard and found a jar of the popular Australian spread
and held it out to Peter.

'Is this what you want?'

'Yes,' he said. 'Dynamite bread.'

She flashed a triumphant smile Jonno's way and one of his eyebrows quirked high but he didn't smile back.

'One dynamite sandwich coming up,' she said, and in spite of Jonno's grimness she gave herself a mental pat on the back for passing her first test in Childspeak.

But her stomach was such a bunch of knots she couldn't bring herself to eat lunch. She served up a slice of the quiche and a salad for Jonno, but left him to eat on his own while she took Peter to the bathroom for a wash and then made his lunch.

The little boy was worn out after his long horse ride in the heat, so by the time he'd finished his Vegemite sandwiches and milk he was happy to be settled for a nap on a daybed on the shady back veranda.

Camille wondered what would happen now. Would Jonno order her to leave again, just as he had last night? She felt wretched and ill when she heard his footsteps coming through the house towards the kitchen.

'Camille.'

Her head snapped around. He stood behind her with his thumbs hooked over the belt of his jeans, looking stern.

'We've got to talk.'

Her mouth was so dry she had to pass her tongue over parched lips before she could reply. 'Yes, I guess we do.'

'I know you probably meant well by coming here, but believe me it's not wise.'

Her breath shuddered on a nervous sigh. This was so

ironic. She'd been quite sure that coming to Edenvale was the wisest and bravest decision of her twenty-seven years and here was Jonno telling her she'd been foolish.

Her eyes stung, but dissolving into tears wouldn't help her prove to this man that she was a stronger person than he suspected, so she tilted her chin and eyed him as bravely as she could. No doubt she looked haughty, but at least that was better than looking tearful.

'What are you saying, Jonno? Are you telling me that it's OK for you to turn up on my doorstep without warning whenever the mood takes you, but it's no good if the boot's on the other foot?'

He glared at her. 'Circumstances have changed.'

'Yes, they have.' She pushed her shoulders back and took a deep, deep breath. 'And so have I.'

He looked startled. 'What do you mean?'

'I'm not the girl I used to be.' She tried for a smile. 'I—I seem to have grown up.'

Harsh colour came and went in his face as he stared at her. 'Grown up? What are you talking about?'

'I'm talking about your son and how I want to help you look after him.'

A jolt of electricity seemed to arc through Jonno. He gripped the back of a nearby chair with white-knuckled hands and scowled, dark brows arrowing together. He shook his head. 'It's not going to work.'

'Why not?' she cried. 'I'm willing, and Peter seems to like me.'

'Peter's already had enough turmoil in his short little life. He doesn't need you to blow in, win his heart and then blow out again.'

She spun away from him so he couldn't see how much his assumption hurt her. 'This is kind of embarrassing,' she said to the line of red and white mugs hanging from hooks on the pine dresser. 'You seem to be able to barge into my life in Sydney or Paris and say abracadabra and I'm yours. I thought I'd be able to walk in here and look into your eyes and—and you'd *know*.'

From behind, she heard him take a step towards her and then hesitate. 'I guess I must be slow,' he said in a voice that was rough and scratchy. 'So spell it out for me, Camille. What should I know?'

She dragged in another deep breath and looked back at him over her shoulder. Oh, heavens! This was awful. Jonno looked as scared as she felt. 'I'm trying to tell you—that—that I don't want to do the stay-in-Sydney, no-marriage-no-kids thing any more.'

He didn't speak. Just stood still as a poised panther, watching her with fierce eyes. Her heart gave a frightened, hopeless bound, then seemed to stop completely. If she couldn't make Jonno understand all was lost.

Drawing on her last shreds of courage, she turned around so they were face to fearsome face. 'I've walked through a door, Jonno. Like Alice through the looking glass. I've arrived at another place and I can't go back. I've fallen in love with you. I truly love you. The real thing. Better than sex. More than sex. I want to be able to help you with Peter and I want to be with you both forever. And I—'

Suddenly, without warning, she was crying. She was babbling and crying and she couldn't go on talking and she couldn't see Jonno through her tears.

But it didn't matter, because he was holding her. His arms were around her and he was crushing her against him and he was murmuring her name over and over as he pressed his lips to her forehead, her nose, her damp cheeks and eyelids.

'Camille,' he whispered. 'Camille, don't cry, sweetheart.'

'But you don't want me any more,' she spluttered.

'I do. I do.' His hand pressed her head onto his shoulder and he buried his face in her hair. 'Of course I want you. I've always wanted you, Camille, and I want you now more than ever.'

It was so good to be in his arms again. She slipped her hands around his neck and clung to him.

'Problem was, I just didn't know how you felt,' Jonno added. 'You were so determined to stay independent.'

'I was fooling myself.'

He pressed warm kisses into her neck. 'You were afraid.'

'Yes, I was,' she whispered against his comforting shoulder. 'I was a coward.'

He stroked her hair. 'You've never been cowardly, darling. You had good reason to hold back after seeing your parents' unhappiness.'

She lifted her tear-stained face so she could look at him. 'But I've learnt things from my parents, Jonno. I was worried about our differences and the fact that we had so little in common. Then I realised that my mother and father had everything in common. They had their love of dancing, their partnership, their touring together—and none of it saved their marriage.'

A sob escaped. 'They're still miserable, Jonno, because they haven't had the courage to admit their mistakes. So that's why I'm admitting to you I was wrong. I was so, *so* wrong. I want to commit and—I—I really think I could learn to be quite good with children.'

He was smiling at her with his lovely half-grin. 'You're already brilliant with Peter.'

'It's so easy to love him. He's so like you. I'm quite sure I adore him already.'

'He's kinda cute, isn't he?'

'He's a darling.' After a moment she added, 'And I want to raise cattle.'

Jonno pulled back in surprise. 'Really?'

She looked up at him with a sniffling, shy smile. 'I want to buy more steers, and this time I want to stay here to watch them grow every step of the way.'

Shaking his head in bewildered amusement, he asked, 'And what about your job at *Girl Talk*?'

'I've already resigned.'

'Camille!'

'Well, I haven't totally resigned. I've arranged to freelance for them. From here. Have laptop—will write.'

'And you organised all this behind my back?' He didn't sound as if he minded at all.

'Yes. I rang Edith from Paris.'

'And she agreed?'

Camille shrugged. 'I didn't give her much choice.' Slipping her hands from around his neck, she reached for his hands and held them in front of her as she looked straight into his warm hazel-green eyes. 'But I'm giving you some choices, Jonno. This time I'm the one making the big offer. We can do this any way you like.'

Quick moisture shimmered in his eyes as his thumbs massaged the backs of her hands. 'Any way I like?'

'As long as I can stay here with you and Peter and as long as it involves forever.'

He drew in a long, shuddering breath and her heart stumbled. Her big, manly cattleman looked as if he might cry. 'What—what if I asked you to marry me?' he said.

Oh, my God, would he? Her knees began to knock. 'I think I'd be inclined to say yes.'

'You *think* you'd be *inclined…*?'

'Why don't you ask me and find out?'

His smile was the shy, quirky grin of a nervous boy. 'Camille, this sounds crazy, but can you wait just a minute?'

'I—I guess so.'

Without another word he hurried out of the kitchen while Camille pressed hands to her heated cheeks and tried not to panic. This was not a bad sign. OK, so the man she was desperately, deeply in love with had been about to propose marriage and then disappeared at the vital moment, but it wasn't a drama.

Stay calm, Camille. Deep breaths. Think yoga. Believe!

To her relief he was back before she could make herself too sick with worry. And he was carrying a cute little red box tied with a white satin ribbon.

'I took this to Paris,' he said. 'To be honest, I wanted to ask you to marry me there.' He shot a rueful smile towards the dirty dishes in the sink. 'I know this old kitchen isn't exactly the Eiffel Tower or the banks of the Seine.'

'It's fine, Jonno. It's fine.' Everything was fine.

He placed the box in her shaking hand. 'You've no idea what you mean to me,' he said. 'I love you more than anything on this earth. That's why I didn't want to ask you to give up Sydney or your job or your independence.'

'Stop worrying,' she said. 'Falling in love has been such an eye-opener for me. I had no idea it could change me so much. I don't want anything as much as I want you, Jonno. I don't want to have to breathe without you.'

The skin around his eyes creased as he grinned. 'If you have no alternative, you take a gamble.'

'Except that this time there's no gamble. I'm sure I'm on to a good thing.'

His response was to frame her face with his hands and to take her mouth with a slow, deep, tummy-tumbling, heart-stirring kiss.

Some time later he asked, 'Are you going to open this?'

'Oh, yes.' She slipped the satin ribbon from the box and lifted the lid. 'Oh, Jonno,' she whispered when she saw the beautiful ruby and pearl ring in a delicate old gold setting. 'What a gorgeous ring. I love it.'

'As soon as I saw this, it seemed perfect for you,' he said, taking it from her and slipping it onto the third finger of her left hand.

Suddenly he went still and his eyes locked with hers

as he held the ring in place. 'I love you with everything I have, Camille. Will you marry me?'

'Oh, yes,' she said, smiling up at him through a mist of happy tears. 'Yes, Jonno, yes, yes, yes.'

EPILOGUE

From the desk of *Girl Talk*'s Editor.

Dear readers,

Wedding bells have been in the air for the past year as Girl Talk*'s heartthrob bachelors have headed for the altar. Last month another of these heroes bit the dust.*

You'll all remember Jonno Rivers! He was our drop-dead sexy outback bachelor from Mullinjim in North Queensland and we regretfully reported last year that he'd withdrawn from the challenge halfway through the chase.

Well, it's confession-time here at Girl Talk*.*

Sorry, girls, but the true goss on this is that one of our staff members snaffled the scrumptious Jonno for herself.

The lucky woman is Camille Devereaux, and oh, boy, is she one happy chick!

None of the wedding watchers at Girl Talk *has ever seen a bride head down the aisle with such a tear-free, fear-free, stress-free smile. And, believe me, we've seen our share of brides over the past twelve months!*

Jonno and Camille sealed their love by marrying at sunset in a tiny wooden church in the outback township of Mullinjim. Heard of it? You should take a look some time. It has that olde-worlde, rus-

tic charm that you can't find in the city any more.

But there was nothing old-fashioned about our bride and groom. Camille looked sophisticated and absolutely breathtaking in ivory silk and chiffon— the gown of her dreams. And Girl Talk *staffer Jen Summers made a ravishing bridesmaid in navy silk.*

It brings a lump to the throat just thinking about the simple, heartwarming ceremony in that tiny bush church. Jonno and Camille exchanged beautiful vows they'd written themselves and a unique touch was provided when acclaimed musician William Tudmara filled the church with the spine-tingling, amazing sound of the didgeridoo. We were rapt!

And what made the day especially poignant for Camille was that, after years of separation, her father travelled all the way from Paris and her mother came from Tokyo to join her for her big day, and the two of them left together, arm in arm!

Now, while those of us who missed out on grabbing one of Girl Talk's *gorgeous bachelors are feeling distinctly depressed, there is good news for future generations. Jonno's little son, Peter, is a guaranteed heartthrob in the making.*

But for those who can't hang around twenty years or so, waiting for him to grow up, we spied some of Jonno's great-looking single male friends among the wedding guests. That's right. You heard me. There are more heartthrob bachelors where Jonno came from. So don't give up hope.

Till next month,

Edith King

Editor

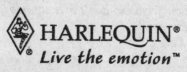

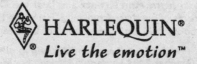

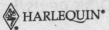

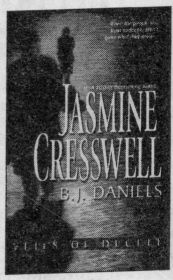